What the Sea Teaches Us
The Crew of the *Morning Light*

By Jeff Kurtti

Foreword by
Roy E. Disney

DISNEP
EDITIONS

New York

An Imprint of Disney Book Group

Academy Award® and Oscar® are registered trademarks
of the Academy of Motion Picture Arts and Sciences.

Emmy is a registered trademark of the Academy of
Television Arts and Sciences.

IMAX® is a registered trademark of IMAX Corporation.

The author would like to sincerely thank and acknowledge
the following individuals for their considerable
contributions of support, encouragement, knowledge,
and expertise to the creation of this book: Sam Claypool,
Leslie DeMeuse Disney, Roy E. Disney, Wendy Lefkon,
Morgan Sackett, and Jessica Ward.

The book's producers would like to extend special
thanks to: Sharon Krinsky, Guy Cunningham, Marybeth
Tregarthen, Sara Liebling, and Tim Palin.

For information address Disney Editions,
114 Fifth Avenue, New York, New York 10011-5690.
Editorial Director: Wendy Lefkon
Senior Editor: Jody Revenson
Assistant Editor: Jessica Ward

Designed by: Jon Glick, mouse+tiger

Photography by: Phil Uhl, Sharon Green, Leslie DeMeuse
Disney, Roy E. Disney, Doug Gifford, Diana DeMeuse,
Robbie Haines, and Abner Kingman.

Photographs on pages 16–19 reprinted with permission
of Bishop Museum Archives.

Library of Congress Cataloging-in-Publication Data on file

ISBN 978-14231-0727-9

First Edition
10 9 8 7 6 5 4 3 2 1
Printed in Singapore

TABLE OF CONTENTS

Foreword

Casting Off

A Greeting from Roy Edward Disney

I took up sailing in 1956 and raised four children on and off the water, doing mostly weekend cruising. But before long, I was bitten by the racing bug. We first raced to Hawaii in 1975, on the S & S yawl *Shamrock*, and have successfully participated in every Transpac since, even setting new elapsed time records in 1977 and 1999. Those who follow such things know I've had a succession of boats, each named *Pyewacket*, and have been an enthusiastic offshore racer for nearly two decades. We've won a lot of races, set some records, and once, we won the World's Maxi Championship, back in 2004.

The sea is a stern teacher, and along the way I've learned a lot about competition, the importance of teamwork, good communication, reliance in self, trust in others, and what the sea teaches us all about patience, perseverance, and just plain luck.

This book is a brief chronicle of one of the best crews I've known, for the seemingly simple reason that they came together from fifteen different directions and became one. The *Morning Light* idea was a straightforward one: to recruit, train, and put to the test fifteen young sailors (average age of 21.2 years) as—on their own—they raced a Transpac 52 called *Morning Light* to Hawaii. None were actors. There was no script and no preconceived outcome.

I hope that in this book you will get to know the individual personalities and distinctive characteristics that brought these young people to *Morning Light*, and will accompany them on their individual emotional, educational, and spiritual journeys—from the selection process and a unique improvisational training program, through sea trials, and on to the completion of the 2007 Transpac race.

—Roy E. Disney

FIRST
LEG

A Race Apart

A Brief History of the Transpacific Yacht Race and Its Ships

With forty-four races since 1906, the Transpacific Yacht Race to Hawaii is well into its second century as the longest of the two oldest ocean races in the world. The race was inspired by King Kalakaua, the revered Hawaiian leader of the late nineteenth century, who believed that such an event would strengthen the islands' economic and cultural ties to the mainland. But it didn't happen until after Kalakaua's death, when Clarence MacFarlane, a Honolulu racing sailor and friend of the king, invited several contemporaries from San Francisco and Los Angeles to race to the Hawaiian Islands. The race was scheduled to start in the early summer of 1906, but

when MacFarlane sailed his 48-foot schooner into San Francisco Bay he realized there would have to be a change of plans. The city lay in ruins following the great earthquake twenty-seven days earlier.

But MacFarlane wasn't easily discouraged. He changed the starting point to Los Angeles, and except for one nostalgic return to San Francisco for the start in 1939, the race has started from the Los Angeles area ever since. The finish is off the Diamond Head lighthouse just east of Honolulu, 2,225 nautical miles from the starting line.

ABOVE: **Transpac founder Clarence MacFarlane, who sailed his schooner *La Paloma* in the first race in 1906.**

RIGHT: **Harold Dillingham's 60-foot schooner *Manuiwa* won the Transpac in 1934.**

The Competitors and Their Prizes

The 2007 race was the forty-fourth Transpac. Through its 100-year history, it has been sailed by 1,700 boats from 17 countries, including 124 foreign competitors. The race is run biennially in odd-numbered years, alternating with the Newport-to-Bermuda race that also started in 1906.

The fastest in the fleet have traditionally competed for the Transpacific Yacht Club Perpetual Trophy, which is better known as the "Barn Door" because of its unique size. It is a three-and-a-half-by-four-foot plaque of hand-carved Hawaiian koa wood bearing the words "First to Finish." This title isn't necessarily accurate anymore—since 1991 the starts have been staggered. The slower boats start a few days ahead of the faster boats in order to compress the finishes and facilitate celebrations in Hawaii—and occasionally one will finish before the later, faster starters. Thus, in keeping with tradition, the "Barn Door" is awarded to the monohull with the fastest elapsed time.

Smaller and/or slower boats unable to match the larger, faster ones in sheer speed compete for a prize more relevant to crew performance: the King Kalakaua perpetual trophy for the best corrected-handicap time. Each boat's speed potential is calculated from a rating system that takes into account a multitude of statistics, including the boat's length, weight, and sail area. This rating is factored into an equation, along with the time and distance of the race, in order to reward the crew that sailed its boat nearest to its peak performance. The overall winner also receives the take-home Governor of Hawaii trophy, a hand-carved model of a Hawaiian sailing canoe.

Adorned with leis, skipper Richard Rheem and his crew celebrate their victory aboard *Morning Star*; they were the first to finish the 1953 Transpac.

Yachts tie up at Ala Wai harbor following the completion of the Transpac, circa 1957.

Port of Departure

Since 2005, the city of Long Beach has served as Transpac's mainland home port, and the race has become a highlight of the city's annual Sea Festival celebration. In 2007, the city's Department of Parks, Recreation, and Marine funded and placed along the harbor's edge eleven historical monuments chronicling each decade of the race in text and photos.

Now, instead of simply showing up at the starting line and sailing away, Transpac racers gather at complimentary moorings in Rainbow Harbor in downtown Long Beach for a week or more before their starts, enjoying camaraderie and adjacent attractions such as Shoreline Village, the Aquarium of the Pacific, restaurants, and shopping. From there, following spirited ceremonial send-offs when each boat and its crew is introduced to the throngs on the surrounding promenades, they proceed eight miles west to Point Fermin for their starts, and the race is on.

Merlin, a Santa Cruz 68 designed by Bill Lee, won the Transpac in 1977, setting a record that would hold for twenty years. Skipper Dan Sinclair sailed *Merlin* to victory again in 1995 (ABOVE) placing first overall on corrected time.

Pacific High

Transpac stands apart from other major ocean races as essentially a downwind race, determined by normal weather patterns in the eastern Pacific north of the equator. But the most successful boats seldom sail a straight line to Hawaii, instead taking a southerly course to avoid the Pacific High, a region of high pressure (and thus light winds) rotating clockwise between Hawaii and the West Coast of North America. After two or three days of sailing against the wind, they come into the warm, following trade winds. Spinnakers go up, shirts come off, and sailors traditionally enjoy a faster and more pleasant ride the rest of the way.

Oddly, it wasn't until the second half-century of the race, following World War II, that competitors discovered this phenomenon and used it to their advantage in charting their courses and optimizing their boats for downwind performance. But the race remains a navigational challenge. While the smart call has been to sail a longer course looping farther south into stronger breeze, thus sailing farther but faster, the trick is not to sail so far south as to experience diminishing returns.

In recent years, that strategy led to the evolution from traditional, heavy, oceangoing yachts to the new breed of lightweight flyers: first, ULDB 70 "sleds," so-called for their "downhill" performance; and then the maxZ86s and other long, skinny, and ultralight speed burners that led a record assault in 2005.

Records and Racers

The current monohull record holder is *Morning Glory*, a Reichel/Pugh–designed maxZ86 owned by industrial software magnate Hasso Plattner of Germany. *Morning Glory* led the way in 2005 with an elapsed time of six days, nineteen hours, four minutes, and eleven seconds, knocking nineteen-and-a-half hours off the record set by the third of Roy E. Disney's *Pyewackets* in 1999. The Director Emeritus and consultant to The Walt Disney Company (son of Disney co-founder Roy O. Disney, and Walt Disney's nephew) was only two-and-a-half hours behind on his fourth *Pyewacket*, also an R/P maxZ86, in his fifteenth Transpac.

Since allowing multihulls to compete, the fastest elapsed time is not necessarily earned by a monohull. Steve Fossett's sixty-foot trimaran *Lakota* raced the course in six days, sixteen hours, seven minutes, and sixteen seconds in 1995, well under the monohull record at the time of 8:11:01:45 by the ultralight displacement "sled" *Merlin* that stood for twenty years. Then, in 1997, Bruno Peyron's 86-foot catamaran *Explorer* smashed Fossett's record with a time of five days, nine hours, eighteen minutes, and twenty-six seconds.

The largest boat ever to race the Transpac was the 161-foot *Goodwill*, whose best time was ten-and-a-half days in 1959. The smallest boat was the twenty-five-foot B-25 named *Vapor*, sailed doublehanded by Bill Boyd and Scott Atwood of Long Beach in 1999. Size is now artificially restricted by imposing "speed limit" ratings on all entries through evaluation of potential performance.

The Transpac is one of only six races listed as Ocean Classics in the book, *Top Yacht Races of the World*. It remains a race for boats large and small, and sailors amateur and professional, with perhaps the most desirable and romantic destination of all.

—Courtesy of the Transpacific Yacht Club
www.transpacificyc.org

Roy E. Disney's *Pyewacket* surfs through the Molokai Channel at 25.8 knots during the 2007 Transpac.

What the Heck is a Pyewacket?

Pyewacket was a spirit that convened with witches and was detected by the "witchfinder general" Matthew Hopkins in March 1644 in the town of Maningtree, Essex, UK. Hopkins claimed he spied on the witches as they held a meeting close by his house. The incident is described in Hopkins's pamphlet *The Discovery of Witches* (1647).

In the 1950 play and the 1958 movie, *Bell, Book and Candle*, Gillian Holroyd's Siamese cat is named Pyewacket. The name has become a fairly popular one for cats because of this story, but relatively few people know its origin.

Pyewacket is also the current name of a maxZ86 class sailing yacht commissioned in 2004 by Roy Disney, designed by Reichel-Pugh along with an identical sister ship named *Morning Glory*, and built in the Cookson shipyard in Auckland, New Zealand. The boat is a modern turbo sled, equipped with a hydraulic canting keel, which allows it to shift its keel-ballast in order to reach previously unthinkable speeds. In 2004, she was Maxi-boat World Champion, sailing in Sardinia. In 2005, following a record passage to Honolulu in the Transpac, the boat was donated to Orange Coast College as a sail training vessel. In 2006, she was leased back to Roy Disney and highly modified especially for the 2007 Transpac, with the addition of eight feet to the length of the hull, ten feet to the height of the mast, and a number of other go-fast modifications.

There were three previous *Pyewackets*, each faster than the last, beginning with a 67-footer and progressing to a 75-footer. The last two each set a number of records in distance racing in the Pacific, the Great Lakes (Chicago-Mackinac), and the Atlantic, as well as winning numerous regattas. Some of those records still stand.

LEFT: **In the 2007 Transpac, *Pyewacket* would go on to finish with the fastest elapsed time, winning the prestigious Barn Door trophy.**

23

2

The *Morning Light* Project

A Background on the Origin of the Idea and the Establishment of the Project

Along with the styles of the competing boats, the face of the Transpac race itself has evolved with the times. Since 1979 there have been all-female crews, and in 1997 there was a crew composed entirely of men with HIV and AIDS, who carried a message of hope on the horizon for a cure for the disease. In 2003 and 2005 a team of disabled sailors, representing Challenged America of San Diego, sailed a Tripp 40 called *B'Quest*. Double-handed crews have been recognized since 1995, and 2005 saw a record of seven double-handed entries, including the first all-woman duo, Patricia Garfield and Diane Murray, and the first coed team, James and Ann Read (with their dog, Sweetie Pie). The Reads, who were in no hurry, logged the slowest race time ever from Los Angeles to Honolulu: twenty-two-and-a-half days.

(Both of those entries raced in the Aloha class, which was introduced in 1997 to accommodate boats that, while older, heavier, or blessed with interior comforts ranging from air conditioning to big-screen TVs, still wanted to race to Hawaii. They may not use their auxiliary engines, but may use power-assisted winches and other aids.)

Crew members have been as young as eleven years old. The two youngest crews in Transpac history competed in 2007. Brothers Sean and Justin Doyle sailed their father Dan's boat, a 1D35 renamed *On the Edge of Destiny*. The five young men onboard ranged in age from seventeen to twenty-three, with an average age of just under twenty years.

The second was a team of fifteen sailors (including four alternates), ages eighteen to twenty-three, with an average age of 21.1, sailing a Transpac 52 called *Morning Light*.

—Courtesy of the Transpacific Yacht Club
www.transpacificyc.org

The Dawn of *Morning Light*

"The idea came to us by way of a good friend named Tom Pollack," Roy Disney recalls. "Tom is president of the TP52 association and is forever out there trying to promote the class. He came to us knowing that Leslie and I are filmmakers and said, 'Why don't you do a movie about the youngest crew ever to do the Transpac—and do it on a TP52?' And that idea really is where this all started. It just seemed like a good idea."

The initial aim was to have a crew younger than the seven young men who sailed on Jon Andron's victorious Cal 40 *Argonaut* in the 1969 Transpac. That crew averaged 22.57 years of age. Two of the crew members were seventeen, but the minimum age for *Morning Light* would be eighteen. "Any applicants not eighteen by January 1, 2007, were not eligible," sailing team manager Robbie Haines said.

Another priority was diversity. Haines said, "We were looking for a crew totally inclusive concerning race and gender." About 200 of the 538 applications were from young women, and many others were from various minorities.

Roy Disney continues, "The idea originally was to be the youngest crew ever to do Transpac, and we did a lot of research, actually sailed with some people who were on the boat that had the youngest crew ever to win Transpac. They had an average age of about twenty-two, and they had a thirty-eight-year-old navigator who brought the average way up. So we were aiming for a crew that was going to average twenty-one, or twenty-one-and-a-half.

As it turned out, the five young men sailing *On the Edge of Destiny* would have an average age just one year younger than the *Morning Light* crew, earning them the "youngest crew" accolade upon their completion of the 2007 race. "The initial concept obviously determined how we recruited the crew for the boat," Roy Disney explains, "and then gradually, as we got to know the kids more and more, that whole 'youngest crew ever to do the race' thing got to be less and less important. What got to be more and more important was the kids themselves, and who they were, and how they were going to learn to cooperate and become a team. Which I think is a much more interesting story anyway."

Judges Roy E. Disney, Leslie DeMeuse Disney, and Robbie Haines wanted a crew of diverse, experienced, young sailors to race the *Morning Light*.

In 1951, Roy graduated with a Bachelor's degree in English from Southern California's Pomona College, and soon launched his entertainment career as an assistant film editor on the television series *Dragnet*, starring Jack Webb. He joined The Walt Disney Studios in 1954, working as an assistant editor on the successful True-Life Adventure films, including *The Living Desert* and *The Vanishing Prairie*, both of which won Academy Awards. He later wrote and co-produced *Mysteries of the Deep*, which won an Oscar nomination in 1959.

Roy also wrote for television series, including *Walt Disney's Wonderful World of Color* and the popular *Zorro*, starring Guy Williams. Then, in 1964, he formed his own production unit, writing, producing, and directing some thirty-five other television and theatrical productions, including *Varda, the Peregrine Falcon*; *Mustang!*; *The Owl That Didn't Give a Hoot*; and *Pancho, the Fastest Paw in the West*. He joined the Company's Board of Directors in 1967.

After twenty-three years, Roy left the Studio in 1977 to become an independent producer and investor, but he returned seven years later to serve as the Company's vice chairman and head of the animation department. During his tenure, Disney animation produced some of its greatest box office successes of all time, including *The Little Mermaid*, *Beauty and the Beast*, and *The Lion King*.

Roy literally combined the Company's past with its future when he revived one of his uncle's most colorful visions. *Fantasia 2000*, a continuation of Walt Disney's 1940 classic *Fantasia* that combined classical music with original animation, rang in a new millennium on January 1, 2000, at IMAX theaters across the country.

In 2004, Roy was nominated for an Academy Award in the Best Short Film, Animated category as producer of *Destino*, the realization of a Salvador Dali short subject that the renowned surrealist had begun at the Disney Studio in 1948. Roy currently serves as a consultant for The Walt Disney Company and Director Emeritus for the Board of Directors

Roy E. Disney

Roy E. Disney is the son of Roy O. Disney and nephew of Walt Disney, the Company's founders. Born in Los Angeles on January 10, 1930, Roy practically grew up at the Studio, where his father managed business affairs, while his uncle inspired artists to create magical animated worlds for movie screens. Roy was there when *Snow White* and *Pinocchio* were born and once recalled, "The animators used to test stuff out on me. They'd say, 'Come on in and watch this and see if you think it's funny.'"

Leslie DeMeuse Disney

Documentarian Leslie DeMeuse Disney grew up racing Lasers on San Francisco Bay, and by the age of fifteen had crewed in her first Transpac race. She earned a Bachelor of Science from the University of the Pacific in business administration with a concentration in marketing. After working on an MBA at Golden Gate University, she studied television production at the American Film Institute. In 1985, she and Phil Uhl formed Channel Sea Television, specializing in yacht-racing coverage. Leslie won an Emmy Award for producing a PBS special on yachting, *White on Water*. For a span of fifteen years, she produced yacht-racing specials for ESPN. In addition, she was a series producer for Prime Sports Net for the America's Cup, and was a segment producer for the ABC/Disney Channel's *American Teacher Awards*. For ten years she has been on the Transpac Board of Directors, and has partnered with filmmaker Roy E. Disney, producing documentary programs, including the DVD on Transpac history, *A Century Across the Pacific*. She has a son, Kenny, who is attending the Jacob School of Engineering at the University of California, San Diego.

3

A Privileged Vessel

A Description of the *Morning Light* Itself

"If we do our job right," Roy Disney says, "I don't care as much whether they win or lose as how they come together as a group and wind up a team in the end. However they do is how they do. But we're giving them the equipment to win."

The *Morning Light* itself is a Transpac 52, designed by Farr Yacht Design and built by Goetz Custom Boats. It is part of the world's most dynamic grand prix class, with more than thirty boats in fifteen countries. It was launched in summer 2005, and Honolulu is its home port.

TP52s are fully-crewed, high-performance monohulls, capable of racing in both buoy regattas and blue water offshore races, and are designed for racing by amateur and professional sailors alike. Upwind, they are stiff and fast, as approximately sixty percent of the weight of the boat is in the metal fin and lead bulb. TP52s do not use water ballast, canting keels, or running backstays, and they can easily exceed twenty-five knots off the wind (the record being thirty-two knots, set by four TP52s racing down the California coast in 2003).

2007 OFFSHORE RACING RULE CERTIFICATE™

USA
52007

YACHT NAME:	**MORNING LIGHT**
SAIL NUMBER:	USA- 52007
ADDRESS:	Mr Roy E Disney
ID: 102435H	4444 W Lakeside Dr
	3rd Floor
	Burbank, CA 91505-4054

Signature: _____

CERTIFICATE#:	US41450	AGE DATE:	6/1/2005
ISSUED DATE:	3/11/2008 2:13:13 PM		
YEAR VALID:	2007		
CLASS:	Transpac 52		
BUILDER:	GOETZ		
OFFSETS FILE:	US31236.OFF	ABS PLAN:	Not filed
MEASUREMENT:	FULL (Meters/Kilograms)		
Freeboard Date:	5/25/2007		
Inclining Data:	5/25/2007		
RIG TYPE:	Sloop		
SPNNAKER TYPE:	Asym on a pole		
KEEL TYPE:	Fixed keel		
PROP INSTALL:	Strutdrive		
PROP TYPE:	Folding		

LOA	15.85	DRAFT	3.176
Rated L	15.460	ECE	0.000
BMAX	4.41	Wet AREA	39.76
Stability Index	137.4	PIPA	0.0057
LPS	138.5	RMC	357.3
CREW	1314	VCGM	-0.760
Frbd Fwd M	1.493	RM2	375.6
Frbd Aft M	1.140	RM20	328.1
SG	1.020	RM40	268.4
SFFP	0.457	RM60	196.6
SAFP	14.691	RM90	111.3
DISP Meas	7622	MWT	298.0
Water Ballast	0	MCG	6.866

Genoa/Spinnakers

IG	22.401		
ISP	22.401		
J	6.532		
LPGenoa	141 %		
FSP	0.000		
JLE	0.000		
JR	0.000		
SPL	7.620		
SL	0.00		
SMW	0.00		
SF	0.00		
ASL	22.35		
AMG	13.22		
ASF	13.70		
A Genoa	107.9		
A Sym	249.4		
A Asym	249.4		

Mainsail Meas.

P	20.422
E	7.470
HB	0.150
MGT	1.82
MGU	3.05
MGM	4.76
MGL	6.18
MDT1	0.15
MDL1	0.32
MDT2	0.12
MDL2	0.19
TL	3.04
MSWgt	54.0
A Main	91.4

Mizzen Meas.

PY	0.000
EY	0.000
HBY	0.000
MGTY	0.00
MGUY	0.00
MGMY	0.00
MGLY	0.00
MDT1Y	0.00
MDL1Y	0.00
MDT2Y	0.00
MDL2Y	0.00
TLY	0.00
EB	0.00
YSD	0.0
YSF	0.0
YSMG	0.0
A Mizzen	0.0

TABLE OF RATINGS

GPH: 456.6

	Time-on-Time (TOT)	6kt	8kt	10kt	12kt	16kt	20kt	24kt	A	B
CLOSED COURSE:	1.207	558.6	467.4	422.7	395.8	361.1	335.6	320.1	1.12717	106.21
WW 60%,LW 40%:	1.205	754.4	618.4	549.4	509.5	462.6	426.8	406.9	1.04414	88.20
WW 50%, LW 50%:	1.205	750.4	612.6	541.8	499.9	448.3	405.5	380.2	1.00234	62.81
Ocean Course:	1.307	699.0	540.5	450.1	389.5	321.3	283.2	257.0	0.92797	3.66
Ocean Non-Spin:	1.203	759.8	587.6	488.4	422.6	349.4	307.6	276.7	0.85043	1.72
Offshore Offwind:	1.230	653.8	523.9	451.6	404.6	342.8	298.7	264.4	0.98907	46.18

Chicago-Mackinac All-Purpose TOT: 1.222 **Chicago-Mackinac Offwind TOT:** 1.230

ET = Elapsed Time   CT = Corrected Time
Time on Distance Scoring: CT = ET - (Rating - Rating Scratch Boat) x Distance
Time on Time Scoring: CT = TOT x ET
Performance Line Scoring: CT = (A x ET) - (B x Distance)

US SAILING.

ABOVE: The *Morning Light*'s ORR certificate enumerates all of her specifications, including draft, overall length, and sail area.

At one time or another, a TP52 has won almost every blue water regatta in existence, including overall wins in the 2004 Bermuda race, and the 2004 Chicago to Mackinac. The last two Transpac races were won on overall corrected time by TP52s, with *Alta Vita* winning in 2003 and *Rosebud* winning in 2005.

In buoy racing, TP52s have earned victories at the 2005 Key West race week, the 2003 Miami SORC, and the 2001–2004 St. Francis Big Boat Series against the best boats in the world.

4

Jockeying for Position

A Recounting of the Application Process

It all started with the selection of thirty young adults from a pool of 538 applicants from around the world.

"We came up with several different avenues for getting the word out," Robbie Haines recalls, "from e-mail addresses, to college sailing teams, to magazines, to newsletters—a bunch of different things. We sent out a questionnaire, and we had more than five hundred people respond, both by e-mail and by regular mail. Then we got together in Burbank and spent days and days reading all the applications and putting them in groups."

The selection process was difficult. Roy, Leslie, and their team of judges were looking for a dynamic group of young sailors who had not only the nautical chops to crew the *Morning Light*, but also the chemistry to create an engaging film. Roy Disney recounts, "It was really, really hard to do because we were trying to find experienced sailors, and we were trying to find diversity. We were trying to find interesting character. I think character played a huge part in a lot of the decisions, because obviously it is a movie and we've got to have some characters that'll be fun and clever—that you'd want to spend an hour and a half with."

Once the thirty were selected, they were brought to Long Beach, California, in July 2006 to test their mettle and skills on four Catalina 37s (limited-production racing boats, shown at right). They were greeted by the *Morning Light* coaches and judges, who would narrow the group to a lucky fifteen.

"We decided that fifteen would be the right number," Haines says, "with ten or twelve on the boat and three alternates."

Tests and Trials

The first challenge was a swim test, and the big surprise was that the applicants had to do two laps—fully clothed. Falling overboard is the most deadly aspect of sailing, and it typically happens with clothing on. Trouble began for applicant Steve Manson on lap two. Other swimmers talked him through his struggle. He was exhausted, and even more, embarrassed. He passed the test . . . but just barely.

For the next week, Robbie Haines, the head sailing coach, split the group among the four identical boats. They were given many challenges, including man-overboard drills, where the judges would throw themselves overboard unexpectedly. Other surprises included sailing blindfolded.

TOP ROW: **The judges considered over five hundred applications before deciding on the thirty candidates who would take part in the trial process.**

MIDDLE: **Falling overboard in the open ocean can be dangerous for even the most experienced swimmer, especially considering the added weight of clothes, shoes, and foul-weather gear.**

BOTTOM ROW: **Man-overboard drills were a safety necessity for the *Morning Light* crew, who had to be ready to contend with swinging booms, tossing spinnaker poles, and rough seas at any time of the day or night.**

"We went through a number of exercises," says Stan Honey. "The first exercise was particularly interesting. We called it the 'shrinking triangle' exercise. We divided the kids into four groups and put each group on a boat. We just took them out on the water, and then there were three marks that were very, very close together and it was blowing eighteen to twenty. And then we suddenly said, 'Okay, leave all those marks to port and just start going around the triangle.'

"Then the kids were suddenly in a situation of 'What do we do?' 'Who's skipper?' 'Who's bow?'

'Who's doing what?' And we said, 'You figure it out.' It was very interesting to watch the kids work among themselves to figure out who's doing what. Then we would take the three marks and we'd pull them closer and closer together so that each of the boats that the kids were sailing was just in a continuous state of chaos."

Aboard each boat, observing, was a judge. Every night after sailing, the judges and executive producers would review and discuss each participant.

"It wasn't easy, because they were all so good," Leslie DeMeuse Disney says.

Robbie Haines

Sailing team manager Robbie Haines began sailing at the age of eight in Coronado, California, with Sabots, Penguins, Solings, and Stars. He graduated from Coronado High School and San Diego State University. Robbie has won seven World Championships in five different classes as well as a gold medal at the Los Angeles Olympic Games in 1984. He has worked with Roy Disney for more than fifteen years, managing his sailing projects, most notably the very successful *Pyewacket* series. Robbie has competed in twelve Transpac races and numerous other offshore races worldwide. He is married and has two children.

SECOND
LEG

5

Crewing Up

A Roster of the Final Fifteen Crew Members

"We really must have touched a nerve out there," Roy Disney says. "It was really hard to pick the 'best' of a really outstanding group of people. There wasn't a turkey in the lot. It made our job twice as hard as we thought it was going to be. I feel bad for the kids who didn't get to go. We would have loved to have taken them all.

"We joked that we should have just bought another boat and taken all thirty of them," Roy says of the *Morning Light* finalists, "because they were all fantastic young people." But the final fifteen *were* selected and began their training.

Chris Branning

Hailing from Sarasota, Florida, Chris was a twenty-one-year-old junior in the U.S. Merchant Marine Academy. Chris was a navigator on the *Morning Light*.

"Yes, sir. No, sir." Repeats everything. When Chris Branning first came to the program, I'd ask him to do something, and of course, he'd repeat it because of his military background. He'd call me Mister Haines, and I'd tell him, "Hey, Chris, Mister Haines is my dad. Don't call me Mister Haines." He's turned out to be an excellent navigator, and he's bright. He's very detail-oriented, and Stan Honey had him pegged very early on as the guy to do the nuts-and-bolts navigating for this trip. —Robbie Haines

Branning's a machine. He has the potential of being a terrific navigator and he's got a mind like a steel trap. —Stan Honey

45

Graham is probably the most popular kid in the crew. In a lot of ways, he's the most fun to chat with, be around. Super smart. Super fit. Very strong. He has the least sailing experience of any of the kids, but he's a real contributor to the whole project and to the whole crew. **—Stan Honey**

Graham Brant-Zawadzki

The twenty-two-year-old from Newport Beach, California, was a senior at Stanford University. Graham was an alternate for the *Morning Light*.

Graham is hilarious. Always thinking and always up in spirits which seem to be uncontrollably contagious at times. Though Graham has only been sailing for two years, his racing ability, acute learning curve, and tenacious attitude seem to outshine his expected level of experience. **—Steve Manson**

Chris Clark

A twenty-one-year-old sailmaker from Old Greenwich, Connecticut, Chris was a junior at the University of Mary Washington. Chris was an alternate for the *Morning Light*.

Clark has an intensity that is perfect for a forward-of-the-mast position. He is definitely one of the strongest members of the team and by far the best swimmer. His skills at sailmaking could come in handy. **—Chris Branning**

Charlie Enright

A senior at Brown University, the twenty-two-year-old Providence, Rhode Island, resident is also a racing coach.

Charlie possesses a wealth of sailing knowledge, a great feel for the ocean, and excellent leadership skills. As the youngest member of the team, I'm naturally inclined to look up to certain members of the team. Charlie is the one who I admire most. —**Mark Towill**

Happy-go-lucky Charlie Enright. He's such a delight to be around—I've never seen him frown at anything. He's always got a joke or an "in-joke" with one of his mates. He's also a damn good sailor and a really good team member. —**Roy Disney**

Charlie Enright. This guy is a firefighter. He can fix just about any bad situation and has a natural leadership quality that stems from his vast experience on big boats. He has dinghy sailing skills that make him a valued tactician. I feel comfortable sleeping down below in any conditions knowing Charlie is on deck. —**Chris Branning**

Jesse is a hard worker with a great personality, but a bull in a china shop on a sailboat. He is a quick learner and can get any job done, and he works really hard. He's come from a little bit of a rough background, and that's even more reason why I think the world of him. He never asks for anything and is always the first at the boat. He'll go far in life. **—Robbie Haines**

Jesse Fielding knows everyone and everything there is to know about the sailing world. He really lives and breathes this sport. Just listening to him talk about the sport of yachting, it's obvious how much respect he has for sailing and especially the people who do it well, and that drives him to do whatever he has to every day to get better. That's why I love sailing with him. It's the most important thing in the world to him and you can't help but feel the same way when you're crewing with him. **—Graham Brant-Zawadzki**

Jesse is always up for any challenge and takes it on wholeheartedly. He pours his heart and soul into everything he does, which makes him that much more of a team player. Jesse is one of the few team members who has the potential to really bring us together as more than a team, but as a family. **—Mark Towill**

Jesse Fielding

A boat worker, sailing teacher, and student at the University of Rhode Island, this North Kingstown, Rhode Island, resident was twenty years old.

He's majoring in college, interestingly, in landscape architecture, so how these two things fit together I'm not really clear, but he goes up the mast and out on the end of the spinnaker pole without blinking.
—Roy Disney

Robbie is from Connecticut, goes to URI, and works on some serious boats. I don't know a lot of other kids who are as stoked on the bow as he is, and I definitely don't know any other as good. Robbie has a good sense of humor. Robbie is as mellow as they come. Robbie likes jam bands. **—Charlie Enright**

Robbie Kane

A twenty-year-old student at the University of Rhode Island and racing sailboat captain from Fairfield, Connecticut, Robbie was the bowman on the *Morning Light*.

Robbie Kane is one of the bravest people I've ever met to do what he does on that spinnaker pole at two o'clock in the morning through the Molokai Channel, ten foot waves, when we hit twenty-nine-and-a-half knots of boat speed. The guy's like ice. **—Chris Branning**

Steve Manson

A twenty-two-year-old sailing instructor from Baltimore, Maryland. Steve didn't make the final crew, but was asked to race aboard *Pyewacket*.

Chris Schubert

A twenty-two-year-old Midshipman First Class at the U.S. Naval Academy, Chris is from Rye, New York.

I never heard a more apt nickname than "Bear" for Chris Schubert. He's just a big, good-natured, wonderful, "pitch in and do it" kind of a guy. Part of the team, loved by all, and respected by all. —**Robbie Haines**

Bear. This guy is a barrel of laughs and a ton of fun. He seems very comfortable on the helm as well as giving it his all on the pedestal. Having Bear on board is an automatic boost to crew morale. —**Chris Branning**

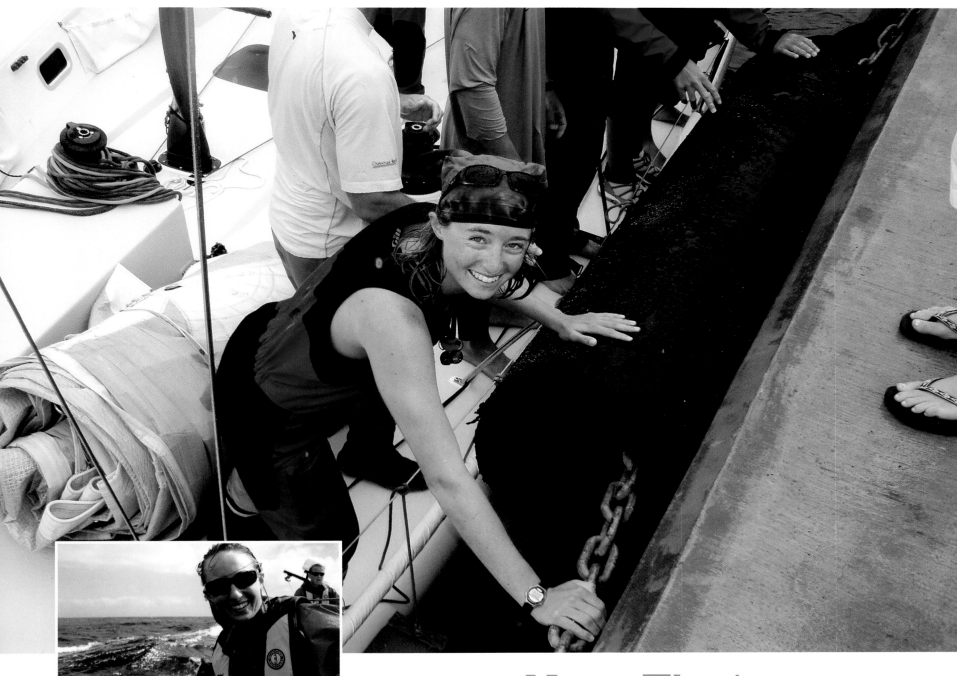

Nobody works harder than Kate, and it was really fun to have her as part of the crew. Every trip out and back she was the one doing all the hardest jobs and all the worst jobs without being asked. Packing the spinnakers, preparing the boat, provisioning the boat, cleaning out the bilge. And people like that, you just can't say enough about them. They're just a treat to have around. **—Stan Honey**

Kate's intelligence and organizational skills constantly amaze me. She's kind of become the team mother and always makes sure that we have enough food, are going to the right place, and are on time for everything. Having grown up on a sailboat, she seems to be quite at ease on the ocean. **—Mark Towill**

Kate Theisen

The twenty-year-old Socorro, New Mexico, resident was a planetary sciences student at New Mexico Tech. Kate was an alternate for the *Morning Light*.

Mark learns so fast. It's really amazing how he can just absorb information and become almost instantly proficient at any task. He doesn't even realize how great he's doing, because his mind is already trying to figure out how he could improve further. —Kate Thiesen

Mark came to us with the reputation of being the oldest eighteen-year-old anybody knew. He's just so mature for eighteen years old. A great leader, a natural sailor, he was born and raised in Hawaii, and he spent a good deal of his life on the water, so he really understands how the water works, and surfing, and sliding around with the boat on the ocean. —Roy Disney

Mark Towill

An eighteen-year-old native of Kaneohe, Hawaii, Towill was a senior at Punahou High School.

Genny Tulloch

A twenty-two-year-old sailor from Houston, Texas, Genny attended Harvard University.

Genny Tulloch is one of the most fun and energetic people I've ever met and probably one of the most competitive. She loves being a leader and has no problem taking the initiative, and with it the responsibility, in difficult situations. But I think she could really benefit by investing a little more in the perspectives, opinions, and goals of the other people she's working with. She's a good friend and a great sailor, and her skills and ambition are going to take her far. —**Graham Brant-Zawadzki**

Genny is very bright, a very good sailor. I was warned ahead of time that she'd be a handful, so I was on the lookout for that. And she was! But there's something there with Genny . . . I think her heart's as good as gold. —**Robbie Haines**

Piet Van Os

This twenty-three-year-old La Jolla, California, native was a senior at the California Maritime Academy. Piet was a navigator on the *Morning Light*.

Welch is one of my favorite people; the salt of the earth, if you will. He comes from Detroit. He lives in a frat at a big state school. Great kid; gets lots of big boat rides. Cleans bottoms; had all his stuff sent to Key West so he could make a few bones while the rest of us spent and were spent. I would go to war with Welch. —Charlie Enright

Chris Welch

From Grosse Pointe Park, Michigan, this nineteen-year-old boat prep and delivery worker was a sophomore at Michigan State University.

Kit's very quiet, bright—has kind of a reserved personality. Little bit hard to get to know, but he's the kind of guy when you're in a team environment, everybody listens to him. He's just the kind of guy that you listen to when he talks. **—Robbie Haines**

Kit is rad. He's an incredibly smart guy and a capable sailor and has a great sense of humor. He's really mellow, which I think some people see as shy. And I really hope that people will see how valuable an asset he is to the team. No matter what seems to happen on the boat, say when we dodge a whale by ten feet and everyone else hesitates, Kit keeps a cool head and gets things done. **—Graham Brant-Zawadzki**

Kit Will

A senior at Connecticut College, the twenty-two-year-old is from Milton, Massachusetts.

Kit's an interesting kid. He might be the first guy on the crew that I would ask to go on a Volvo ocean race because he has all the characteristics of a rock-solid offshore sailor. He's got his eyes open all the time. He's got his mouth shut all the time. He knows what to do. He jumps in and does it quickly. And then when you give him responsibility for something, he owns it. **—Stan Honey**

Jeremy Wilmot

The twenty-one-year-old native of Sydney, Australia, was a sophomore at St. Mary's College of Maryland. He was skipper of the *Morning Light*.

6

Rounding the First Mark

An Account of the Crew's First Acquaintance, Housing, and Training

Now that the initial crew had been selected, they would be relocated to Honolulu, Hawaii, to train in challenging sea conditions. Each would have to take a leave of absence for six months from college, work, and family. This was a small sacrifice for the opportunity to be trained by the finest professionals in the sport of sailing, with state-of-the-art equipment, and in one of the most beautiful and spectacular settings in the world.

"The weather is a lot more dependable in Hawaii," Roy Disney says. "We know we're going to have the trade winds probably ninety percent of the time, and they're big winds, and big seas—and it's harder sailing.

"It's also a lot more pleasant in January to be sailing in Hawaii than in California where it's icy. It gets awfully cold offshore in California, and wet, and rough, and tough on kids, and tough on boats. Tough on grown-ups, too."

LEFT: **Hawaiian navigator and philosopher Nainoa Thompson taught the *Morning Light* crew methods of wayfinding that predate satellites and nautical charts.**

61

A Philosophical Foundation

Over Thanksgiving weekend, the group took their first trip to Hawaii to meet the legendary Nainoa Thompson, a renowned Polynesian navigator and philosopher. Nainoa is well known for challenging and shaping the lives of young people, taking them across the Pacific on the voyaging canoe *Hokule'a*.

He acquainted the *Morning Light* team with the art of navigation by the wind, the waves, and the stars, using methods that his forefathers would have employed centuries ago, when no navigational tools were used.

After two days and two nights sailing with Nainoa, the *Morning Light* crew had gained a new insight about the nature of sailing—and a reverence for ancient Polynesian thinking. They also found a new respect for the sea and its many caprices and uncertainties.

Nainoa Thompson

For the last twenty years, Nainoa Thompson, navigator and sailing master of the Polynesian Voyaging Society's double-hulled canoe *Hokule'a*, has inspired and led a revival of traditional arts associated with long-distance ocean voyaging in Hawaii and throughout Polynesia.

Thompson has reintroduced the ancient system of wayfinding, or non-instrument navigation, synthesizing traditional principles of ancient Pacific navigation and modern scientific knowledge. He is the first Hawaiian and the first Polynesian to practice the art of wayfinding on long-distance ocean voyages since such voyaging ended in Hawaii around the fourteenth century.

Thompson is currently program director of the Polynesian Voyaging Society, where he uses his accomplishments of the past twenty years to develop multi-disciplined, culturally relevant educational programs in partnership with other educational institutions, organizations, and agencies. In a recent *Honolulu Advertiser* poll of Hawaiian households, Thompson was the most well-regarded Hawaiian public figure, with 78 percent of those polled giving him a favorable rating.

He is a member of the University of Hawaii Board of Regents and is on the advisory council of the Ocean Policy Institute. A former U.S. Merchant Marine officer, Thompson is a certified advanced diver, Red Cross lifeguard, and commercial pilot. He is a 1972 graduate of Punahou School and earned a Bachelor of Arts in ocean science in 1986 from the University of Hawaii. His father, the late Myron Thompson, was a former Kamehameha Schools trustee.

—Courtesy of Kamehameha Schools

Crew's Quarters

Next on the agenda was to find a place to house the *Morning Light* crew for six months. It was important for team building and logistical purposes that the crew be housed together—individual housing, apartments, or a hotel would be an impediment to the success of the group's coalescence. The problem was that no one wanted to rent a house to fifteen young adults. (Would you?)

At the last minute, a house on Diamond Head, in sight of the Transpac finish line, was located. It was an appealing shorefront residence especially suited to the needs of the *Morning Light* crew, and one that was accustomed to an unusual gathering of young people with an attendant film crew—this house had been the setting for the 1999 season of the MTV television series *The Real World*.

The house is located southwest of Diamond Head State Monument, in Kahala, Oahu, an upscale neighborhood about ten minutes from Waikiki, known for its varied residential styles, from the quaint to the grand.

"I didn't even really know where we were going to live. When we pulled up in front of the house I didn't even know it at first. I thought we were just pulling over at a beachside park. Turns out we're the house *next* to the park. It's so gorgeous," says Kate Theisen.

There were two buildings on the property. The main house was for the girls and the house moms, Amy and Devon, and also contained the kitchen and dining area. The back house was for the boys . . . all lucky thirteen of them. They were tenants in paradise, living just boat-lengths away from their ultimate goal. "I think I had the best room to see the R-2 buoy," recalls Steve Manson. "I used to look at it every night before I went to bed. I used to just stay out every night like, 'Man, I'm going to pass that buoy one day.'"

Dawning Light

The refitted Transpac 52, now officially named *Morning Light*, was shipped to Hawaii and turned over to the kids, and every minute responsibility to the vessel was now theirs, from the thrill of sailing to the dull routine of maintenance. Each member of the crew enthusiastically embraced their responsibilities.

At the same time, of course, a documentary film of the entire project was in production. Not only were the crew members getting to know each other, their surroundings, and their vessel, they were doing so under the scrutiny of a camera and a production crew.

In a world recently dominated by all manner of "reality media," it is easy to imagine that the *Morning Light* film was simply following in the footsteps of the previous house tenants.

"I really hate that so many people think that this is a reality TV show," Graham Brant-Zawadzki says. "Those shows are built and geared entirely toward entertainment and shock value, with inflated drama and production-driven plot twists. This isn't about hidden motives or surprise endings. This whole project is about us coming together as a team and learning to work together flawlessly, the boat included, regardless of background. We don't have cameras taping our every move or tracking personal relations."

Still, given the uneventful nature of their first sail, the filmmakers may have wished for more ability to manipulate the story. "We were expecting a little more action, maybe a few screw-ups," Leslie DeMeuse Disney says, "at least for our cameras! But, there were no problems at all!"

Ship Shape

The first dramatic crisis the project directors noticed was that their young crew was physically out of shape. It takes a lot of muscle and endurance to sail a TP52, and being in top physical condition is actually a major safety consideration on the open ocean.

The project took on 24 Hour Fitness as a sponsor. They brought a scientific approach to the task of getting the young crew into fighting shape, and they measured not only weight and mass but proportionate body fat—and some of the team members were a bit soft. Personal trainers worked crew members every morning for a solid ninety minutes before they went sailing in the afternoon for another four to five hours.

"We wake up at six-thirty, eat breakfast and make our lunches, and get in the van at seven-fifteen to hit the gym from seven-thirty to nine o'clock," Chris Branning reports. "Boat work from nine-thirty to about eleven or twelve, and we sail hard until four or five, clean up the boat, then off to dinner."

Fuel for the Boilers

The only problem with this ambitious schedule and copious physical activity was that the crew got hungry. Very hungry. "They very nearly ate us out of house and home!" Leslie DeMeuse Disney says, "Our food budget was well over what we had predicted." Steve Manson became legendary at mealtimes; the crew estimated that he ate upwards of 7,000 calories a day—and never gained a pound!

House and Home

Meals and down time at the house made for incredible bonding experiences. Even though there were strict house rules, including a curfew, they never had to be enforced. The crew were too exhausted from their fitness and sailing schedule. They preferred just to hang out at the house, enjoy each other, and rest up—before again rising at the crack of dawn for yet another round of training.

Safety First

The first and most important part of the training was devoted to safety. Each crew member had to earn their lifesaving and CPR certifications, and also their Safety at Sea certifications from U.S. Sailing, the national governing body of sailing in the United States.

The United States Coast Guard generously supported the team's efforts and provided helicopter and manpower for the "rescue at sea" exercises. West Marine provided life rafts, and Chuck Hawley (a nationally known speaker on marine safety and one of five moderators of the U.S. Sailing Safety at Sea seminars for the last ten years) was head instructor for the Safety at Sea program.

Setting Sail

"I think every single time we sent these kids offshore, we were very, very impressed with their performance," Robbie Haines observes. "Here we are sending twenty-one-year-olds out into really rough conditions here in Hawaii, and we were a little tentative at first about who we were going to put on the boat as far as instructors, whether we were going to send them out by themselves.

"The first time we sent the kids around Molokai, I went with them, Stan went with them, and we

just wanted to see how they handled the extreme conditions here in Hawaii. Most of the time we came back really impressed. You know, there was one time they came back where the boat was a mess and we came down pretty hard on them.

Stan, in particular, was very critical of them coming back with the boat looking like that, and every trip after that, the boat came back absolutely spotless."

Training

One of the primary goals of the training process was to familiarize each crew member with every position on the boat so that each sailor would have the potential to perform any number of different jobs. "We did not want to come in initially and brand them with a bowman role or a grinder role or a helmsman role," says Robbie Haines. "We wanted to rotate each one of them out of each individual role on the boat, and I think we came up with eleven jobs. The pit, grinding, trimming, helmsman, navigator, bow, mast, you know, there were a bunch of different categories that we had each one of these kids do over the four months."

By the time of the last session in Hawaii at the end of April 2007, they had been trained in almost every aspect of offshore sailing, with a strong emphasis on navigation, which was taught by the very best, Stan Honey. Stan spent extra time grooming Piet Van Os and Chris Branning, who were emerging as favorites as the team's navigators.

Navigating in and around the Hawaiian Islands was tricky to say the least. The *Morning Light* crew got a run for their money on a three-day sail from Honolulu to Hilo (on the big island) and back. It was a wet ride for the team; they simply never dried out for three days, but they really had the time of their lives. The winds were strong, but they kept the boat under control and unbroken.

Graham Brant-Zawadzki recalls, "The Hilo trip was intense and awesome. The first three days were gnarly. Almost sixty straight hours of pounding upwind, never seeing anything less than fifteen knots, usually over twenty, and even seeing forty-two knots of breeze, which got us going twenty-four knots with a reefed main and a jib."

"On the trip Robbie had me try out a seasickness patch to see how it made me feel. After about thirty-six hours of sailing and no food, I was feeling okay, but not great. When I got off my midday watch, I went below, dried off, and was about to pass out. I was just closing my eyes when all of a sudden I knew I was in trouble. I calmly got up, leaned my head out the companionway, and waited for the inevitable. It was hysterical. I felt fine, but my body just wasn't about to let me keep any food down. I couldn't help but laugh a little bit, and then boom—*Exorcist*-style vomit. I almost cleared the leeward rail!"

7

The Transpac
Approaches

An Account of the
Selection of the Crew

Difficult Decisions

The crew knew from the beginning of the training process that it would be their responsibility to choose the final team who would ultimately participate in the race. Out of the fifteen, only eleven could go—and after weeks of training together and becoming a cohesive unit, this would be an incredibly tough decision.

"I mean, you know, you'd love to be Daddy and make everything happen for them," Roy Disney says, "but they're going to be out there all by themselves, and they have to be the ones to make that decision about who's the leader and who's the worker bee. And it's not something you legislate. It's something *they* have to decide."

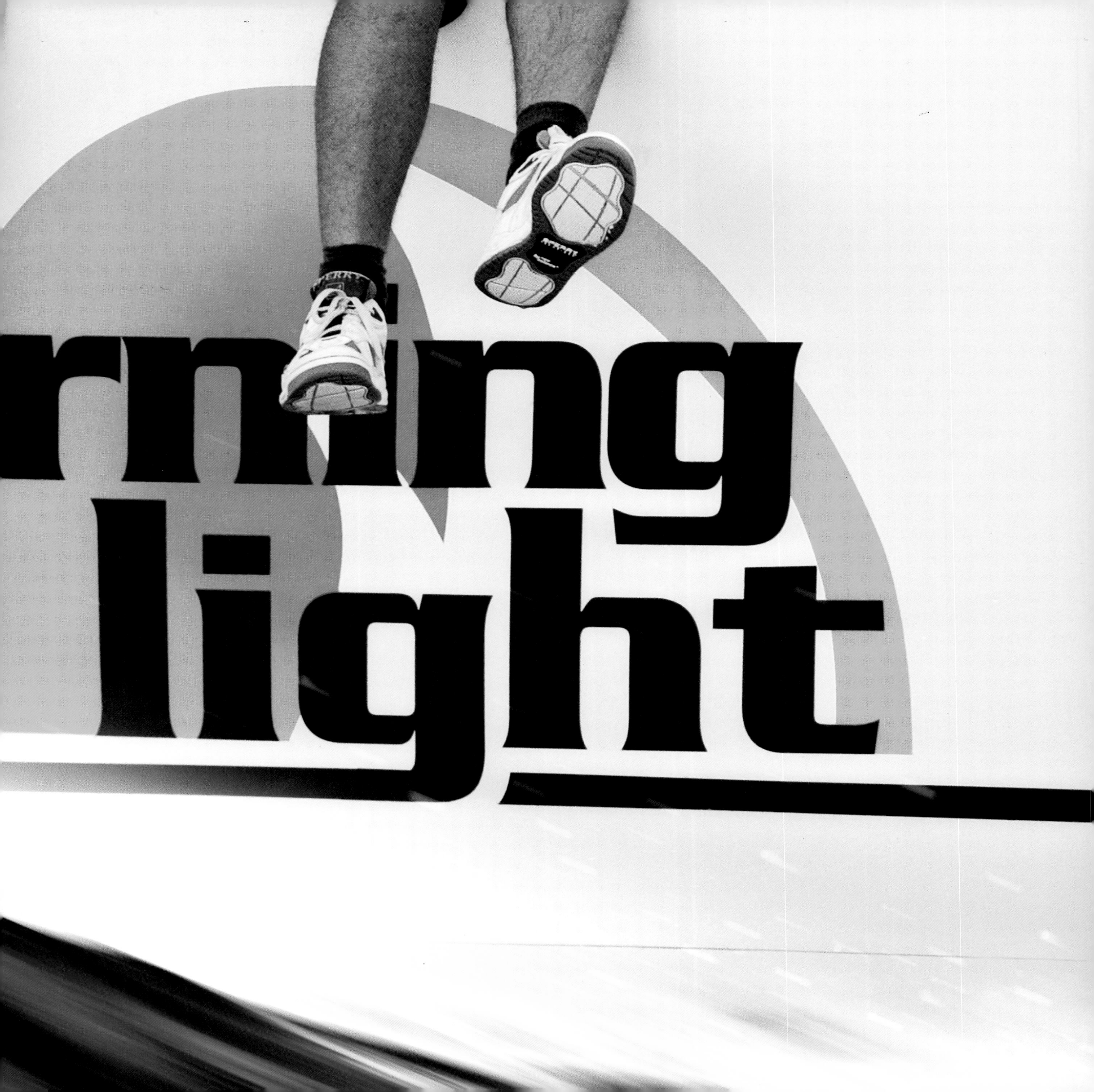
rning
light

Roy continues, "They got together toward the end of the training sessions here in Hawaii and went through among the fifteen of them and chose the eleven who would go in what I thought was a very rational and unemotional way. Although it had to be enormously emotional for all of them."

"The way the kids picked the team," Robbie Haines explains, "is that they unanimously picked Jeremy as the skipper, and then Jeremy picked his team from there. He picked Piet first and then they picked the watch captains, the navigator, and then went down all the way to the final eleven."

"After Jeremy was selected as the skipper, he elected to consult with Piet," Mark Towill recalls. "The two of them began bringing in chosen team members one by one. I can't describe how stressful it was. I was the seventh or eighth person brought into the room."

Kit Will remembers, "I got really nervous once there were only five of us left. We were finally called in and sat down on the floor at the feet of the guys who'd already made it. I remember that the team was joking about something after we were all seated, and I had to bite my lip to keep from expressing my frustration. Just tell us already.

"The expression on Graham's face [when he was the final person picked], words can't describe. Excited disbelief. Everybody in the room was happy for him, and I was, too. I remember smiling as everything seemed to be going in slow motion. The filming lights burned down on me. I couldn't even think. I wasn't disappointed, angry, frustrated—just completely overwhelmed and shocked.

"I didn't understand Jeremy's choice at the time. I don't think I ever will. I know that I wasn't the only one who was surprised by the outcome, but the decision had been made."

The crew roster decided upon that night was comprised of Jeremy, Piet, Genny, Charlie, Mark, Jesse, Chris Schubert, Chris Welch, Chris Branning, Robbie, and Graham, with Kate, Kit, Steve, and Chris Clark acting as alternates.

But it would not be show business without a little drama, and a few weeks later, back in Long Beach, Jeremy decided to make a change in his lineup. He elected to bring Kit aboard, making Graham an alternate. "That was really hard," Roy says. "That was a decision I think Jeremy made because he saw that the boat would be a little faster. And Graham took it hard, but well. Kit looked like the cat that ate the canary for a while, but took it well also. Everybody else did, too. I think the crew saw the reasoning of it."

"Making the decision to bring Kit on the boat was a tough one," Jeremy says, "and it was one that I'd thought about for a long time. I didn't know if I should do it or how I should do it, but at the end of the day I thought I would not be representing the team as the skipper if I didn't take the best crew on the boat."

Kit recalls, "When Jeremy put me on the team, I was completely shocked and totally thrilled that I'd be going on the race, but at the same time, everybody sitting on that boat knew that Graham wouldn't be going and how disappointed he was, and more than anybody I think I know what that disappointment's like."

With the final crew in place, the *Morning Light* team was ready to tackle the Transpac.

Stan Honey

Renowned sailor, navigator, and engineer, Stanley K. Honey, has navigated in fourteen Transpacific races, finishing first six times. Stan holds the monohull records for single-handed and double-handed passages to Hawaii, and he served as navigator aboard *Pyewacket* when it set the record in 1997. In 1996, Stan and his wife, Sally, won the Pacific Cup overall, sailing their Cal 40 *Illusion* double-handed.

Stan co-founded and served as the president and chief scientist of Sportvision, Inc., the leading developer of enhancements for sports TV broadcasts. At Sportvision, Inc., Stan led the development of the yellow first-down line on televised football; the NASCAR race-car tracking and highlighting system; and the baseball K-Zone system, which highlights the pitch location and strike zone in televised baseball.

Prior to co-founding Sportvision, Stan was the executive VP of technology for News Corporation, where he led the development of the FoxTrax system, which tracked and highlighted the hockey puck in televised hockey, and he managed the development of set-top boxes for digital satellite TV, encryption systems, and electronic program guides.

From 1978 to 1983, Stan was a research engineer at SRI International, specializing in radio-location systems, signal processing, underwater sensors, and Over-the-Horizon HF radar.

In 1983, Stan co-founded Etak, Inc., the company which pioneered vehicle navigation and digital mapping. Stan served as CTO, president, and CEO.

Stan is married to Sally Lindsay Honey, a two-time U.S. Yachtswoman of the Year, who has competed in seven 505 world championships and has won the 505 North American championship and the Adams Cup women's sailing championship. She founded and runs Precision Technical Sewing, a twelve person contract sewing and sailmaking company in Palo Alto, California.

8

The Race

A Day-by-Day Descriptive
of the Race Itself

The following chapter is a compilation of official press releases from the Transpac website and journal entries from the *Morning Light* crew. During the course of the race, many factors came into play and many variables changed. Some elements, like wind velocity and barometric pressure, were measurable by those waiting and watching on shore. Other elements, like crew personalities, sleep deprivation, and food rationing, affected the young sailors in ways that only they could reveal.

LONG BEACH, California—It was as if Roy E. Disney's eleventh-hour decision to step off *Pyewacket* sucked the air right out of the final start of the forty-forth biennial Transpacific Yacht Race to Hawaii.

A few hours after his news flashed around the docks at Rainbow Harbor in Long Beach, the fleet

met balmy southeast zephyrs of only three to four knots off the Point Fermin start line in San Pedro that left the high-powered racers gasping for air. With what little wind there was coming from 170 on the compass and the west end of Santa Catalina Island to the right at 215, all 23 boats quickly tacked to port after the gun.

We've been out here for about eight, nine hours now, and we got past Catalina and the wind completely died. Just now we got into about six knots of breeze, which is really a relief. Unfortunately, our competitors might have gotten to it first. But at least we're moving in the right direction toward some more breeze, hopefully a lot of breeze. So for now, we'll just make the boat go as fast as possible.

Our main focus is to try to decide our northern and southern route, depending on the weather files that come in. We just got a new one in that suggests the northern route, which we had almost dismissed as of two hours ago. But now there's a good northern route, and it looks like it may be twelve hours shorter, which is a big deal. **—Piet Van Os**

In the morning when we got the roll call, we found out that we were a little south and west of the fleet, so we're trying to work our way back north and reconnect with the rest of the boats. But everything's going great. The attitude on the boat is awesome. Everybody's spirits are high, and we're all very excited to be here racing.

In ocean racing you get into a rhythm where we do a four-hour watch system. So you're on watch for four hours and then off watch for four. We've all naturally fallen into the rhythm pretty quickly. You know, the first night's really rough, and usually it's kind of scattered and people are trying to get their bearings. But everything's good. I mean, we've done so many offshore practices that it just feels like another day on the water.

It's pretty amazing—last night when the sun went down there were like eight or ten other boats within sight. When we woke up this morning, there was nothing to be seen. Just 360 degrees of blue water and horizon. **—Mark Towill**

July 16, 2007 – DAY 2

LONG BEACH, California—The puzzle that plagues navigators racing to Hawaii is seldom to find the shortest course but the fastest, and this forty-fourth biennial Transpacific Yacht Race to Hawaii has evolved into a classic example.

Pyewacket's Stan Honey said Sunday before the big boats started that he would make the call—north, south, or in between—at "about 6 o'clock tonight," not far past Santa Catalina Island, twenty-two miles off the Southern California coast—and every other eye in the race was on Honey to see which way he'd go. Wouldn't you like to know what the last Volvo Ocean Race winner was thinking?

According to Flagship tracking charts Monday, Honey may have gone conservative. *Pyewacket* was headed generally southwest straight toward the islands, making thirteen knots, with Division 1 rivals Doug Baker's *Magnitude 80* and Mike Campbell and Dale Williams' *Peligroso* falling in behind, well ahead of Bob Lane's *Medicine Man*, which tried the north for a while before dipping back down on a parallel course.

A notable exception was Roger Sturgeon's *Rosebud*, a new STP 65 that flashed impressive speed in two inshore regattas leading up to Transpac. *Rosebud* was headed almost due south at thirteen knots without losing significant distance to its division rivals, except *Pyewacket*, and building leverage for when it turns west into the trade winds.

Not far back was *Morning Light*, a Transpac 52 sailing at 10.8 knots but not as far south as two other Division 2 boats, the Santa Cruz 70s *Westerly* and *Skylark*, streaking side by side at 11.3 knots.

It's day two, late afternoon. It's not nearly as windy as we thought it would be. It's definitely not as cold. We're sailing a great circle route so we're heading a little bit further north. We were trying to get into the most breeze even though it's still going to be less breeze than we wished for. And we've got like fifteen knots right now. We're running at ten knots but not going anywhere super fast. **—Genny Tulloch**

July 17, 2007 – DAY 3

LONG BEACH, California —*Rosebud* and the radically modified *Pyewacket*—essentially, two new, fast, but unknown quantities sailing their first ocean races—appeared to be lining up for a Barn Door showdown on their third day at sea in the forty-fourth biennial Transpacific Yacht Race to Hawaii Tuesday.

Morning roll call positions and Flagship tracking showed *Rosebud*, Roger Sturgeon's STP 65 from Ft. Lauderdale, Florida, had ended its dive into the deep south in quest of favorable breeze and turned west toward the islands, as *Pyewacket*, about two-hundred miles to the north, continued its steady slide directly down the middle of the course, trailed by several other big boats.

It's 17:43, July seventeenth. This morning was pretty tough on the map team. It was really tough on the crew, and they held it surprisingly well. We ended up in two knots of breeze for an hour, and we figured we were going to be shut out the back, passed on both sides.

As the breeze dropped off, normally that's the beginning of a boat falling apart, but everyone held really strong. I woke Piet up from a dead sleep to ask him to go to the top of the rig to see what direction the breeze was going to be coming in.

We're co-navigators, and we give the full brief to Jeremy and he's just as competent as all of us. Then we pulled in Schubert and Charlie because they're our go-to guys as well, and we all looked at it together, and it was a consensus decision.

We basically ended up with the fleet split, and we're going to the north with the northern pack. We all stuck together on that decision. We're still sticking together, and when it's all said and done when we hit the dock, that's really important.
—Chris Branning

We took a gamble. It was a big move at the time. Now we've been fighting for the past two days to get out of it. Now it looks good, then it looks bad, then it looks good. It's not looking too good now, though. Hopefully, we'll get back into the breeze, get the shift, and finally start going downwind. We've got our opponents out to the south of us. They were screaming along with a kite. Guys out to the north of us are in more breeze but just in the same disaster as us.

We did plan on going the southern route. You have this plan for a week, and then all of a sudden like two days out from the race, your plan can just get drastically changed, which ours did. —Jeremy Wilmot

July 18, 2007 – DAY 4

LONG BEACH, California—Just as Roger Sturgeon's new STP 65 *Rosebud* appeared to be lining up on Roy E. Disney's *Pyewacket* with a 297-nautical mile 24-hour run down south a day earlier, dying wind slowed it to only 167 miles before Wednesday's eight a.m. roll call.

At about the same time, *Pyewacket* veered north to get in front of Doug Baker's *Magnitude 80*, which fell in twenty-three miles behind as they continued south-west directly toward Oahu in a twelve-knot nor'easter they hoped was a weak beginning of the trade winds.

But unless the winds increase dramatically, *Pyewacket*'s hopes of reclaiming the elapsed time record of 6 days 16 hours 4 minutes 11 seconds set by *Morning Glory* two years earlier are slim.

Disney, who decided not to sail on the boat the day before last Sunday's start, said from Waikiki, "It's not over yet, but they need to get going. A couple of four hundred-mile days would help."

Good news for Disney was *Morning Light*'s climb to first place in Division 2 in a head-to-head fight

with John Kilroy, Jr.'s *Samba Pa Ti*, another Transpac 52 descending from the north.

Minutes before departing Long Beach for the start line last Sunday, *Morning Light* skipper Jeremy Wilmot reflected on the past year's selections and intense training, with a word for the project's patron, Roy E. Disney.

"We're very ready," Wilmot said. "I'm just eager to get started. We hope we can make him proud."

Okay, so it's day four; lunchtime. It's about 11:30. We just started to crack off the wind so we're going faster. We got the blast reacher up. Everybody's working harder. So it's time to make lunch. Today we've got potatoes and beef with onions. Not my personal favorite but it'll do the trick. It is my personal responsibility to put all the food in the boat, so each day I restock the galley with power bars and fruit and sometimes a little candy to keep everyone happy.

We've got all different kinds of stuff, vitamins and powder for the water which we convert from salt water to fresh so it's sometimes a little nasty. But everything's very weight sensitive. This is a race boat so we use freeze-dried food. It's really lightweight and basically you just add the hot water and give it a good stir and off you go. —**Mark Towill**

Every deck cadet at the academy has to take celestial navigation. During our first year at sea, I spent one hundred days in the Middle East on a container ship and had to do celestial plots, LAN, shooting the sun, the stars. We do the reduction on a computer for this trip to save weight. But we do bring a backup, an almanac book. And in order to save weight we ripped out all the pages of the days that we won't be sailing so we can save half a pound. —**Chris Branning**

HONOLULU—Sometime late Thursday or early Friday the big dogs led by *Pyewacket* will start blowing by *Cirrus*, whose ladies and gentleman won't mind at all. They've already lived their moment in the forty-fourth Transpacific Yacht Race to Hawaii.

"Don't miss [Wednesday's] press release," someone on the boat e-mailed to their fans. "*Cirrus* faster than *Pegasus*! *Cirrus* [sailed] one mile farther than *Pegasus*. You can talk to your grandchildren about this day. Yep, I guess Stan Honey wishes he had Cirrugator on his boat."

But that was when even world-class navigators were struggling in a quagmire of light wind that made this one of the most challenging Transpacs in memory.

Cirrus has no such concerns. Bill Myers's thirty-four-year-old Standfast 40 continues to lead the Aloha B division by more than a hundred miles over the next boat, *Lady Liberty*, the slowest-rated boat in the race. There are no all-women boats in this Transpac but Myers's all-Hawaiian *Cirrus* is close.

"I'm just along for the ride," Myers said. "Lindsey and her mom have taken over the boat. When you're in charge you've got knots in your stomach twenty-four hours a day."

Lindsey Austin, twenty-two, is the skipper who landed on her feet after missing the last cut for Disney's *Morning Light* team.

So it's the night of day five. We've got about fourteen knots sailing downwind with the spinnaker, which is nice. This whole Transpac hasn't really been similar to a typical Transpac. Usually the Pacific high will be really far north and we'd be able to set a spinnaker within the second or third day and go downwind for the majority of time.

This year, the low came through and completely split up the high, so we had to beat really far north, and now we've been sailing upwind for four days—just completely atypical.

It's pretty cool to be out here and know that so many people have made this crossing before us, kind of just following in their wake, craving our own, making our own path, but at the same time it's kind of like a full-circle deal.

For me personally, being from Hawaii, this voyage has a little bit more meaning because in a way, I'm sailing home. Being able to look around and not see any land for a week and then have those islands come out of the horizon can be a pretty special thing.

I was down in my bunk thinking about how much I've learned from this whole trip, and I've realized that there's so much to be learned out here. Being on this boat you're completely isolated, and the ocean can present you with so many different situations and test you a lot with different emotions. There's a lot of scary moments out here, and fear is something you have to learn how to deal with.

When you're on land you can kind of run away from situations, and it's just not possible out here. There's nowhere to go. You have to deal, and in those moments your true personality and your ability to  cope with the elements comes out. The ocean just gives you so many defining moments where you're able to learn more about yourself, and for me that's really valuable. Being out here, I've realized that the journey is more important than the destination. —**Mark Towill**

HONOLULU—Here's where *Pyewacket* stood at Friday morning's position reports for the forty-fourth Transpacific Yacht Race to Hawaii: Barn Door? With a 109-nautical mile lead over Doug Baker's *Magnitude 80*, almost certain. Record? Probably not.

As Roy E. Disney waits in Waikiki, his team is urging all speed possible out of the radically modified 94-foot onetime maxZ86, but even with favorable northeast trade winds kicking in for the second half of the race, that apparently won't be enough to get *Pyewacket* to the finish line off Diamond Head by 2:04 a.m. Hawaii time Sunday and reclaim the record.

Better news for Disney is the ding-dong dogfight for second place in Division 2 between his *Morning Light* team and John Kilroy, Jr.'s *Samba Pa Ti*, both Transpac 52s in lockstep only nineteen miles behind *Holua* and well within sight of each other.

Disney's navigator, Stan Honey, has an interest in both boats. As a coach for the *Morning Light* team of young sailors, he helped to train navigators Piet Van Os of La Jolla, California, and Chris Branning of Sarasota, Florida.

"It is an unusual Transpac," said the man who has won a couple, plus the last Volvo Ocean Race—as has, by the way, Mark Rudiger, his friend and counterpart on *Holua* who navigated Assa Abloy's victory with Paul Cayard in the previous Volvo.

Honey said in a message from the boat: "As far as I can recall, this is the first time in a July race that it was tempting to try to go north of the eastern lobe of the high and cut across the east-west ridge right at the cold front. All navigators that I chatted with were considering such a move but were sensibly frightened by the fact that it was such an unusual approach for a Transpac.

"On the morning of the start we had a combined *Pyewacket* and *Morning Light* weather-and-strategy meeting at which the *Pyewacket* afterguard decided to follow the more conventional southern course.

The *Morning Light* afterguard sounded as if they had decided to take the northern route. When I last spoke to the navigators on *Morning Light* about thirty minutes before the preparatory signal for the start, I confirmed that *Pyewacket* was heading south."

Oops!

Honey continued: "When we analyzed the 18Z GFS model run which we received at 1700 PDT after our start on Sunday, we on *Pyewacket* changed our plan and off we went on the northern course, which looked like it would be very slow in the vicinity of the trough, but if we were able to cross the trough without stopping for too long, the net passage would be as much as twelve to eighteen hours faster than the southern route. It's worth noting that the boats which started earlier really didn't have an attractive option to take the northern course because of the location of the light wind area

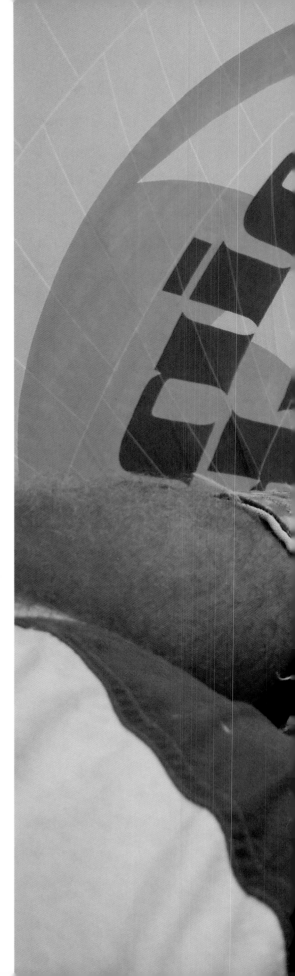

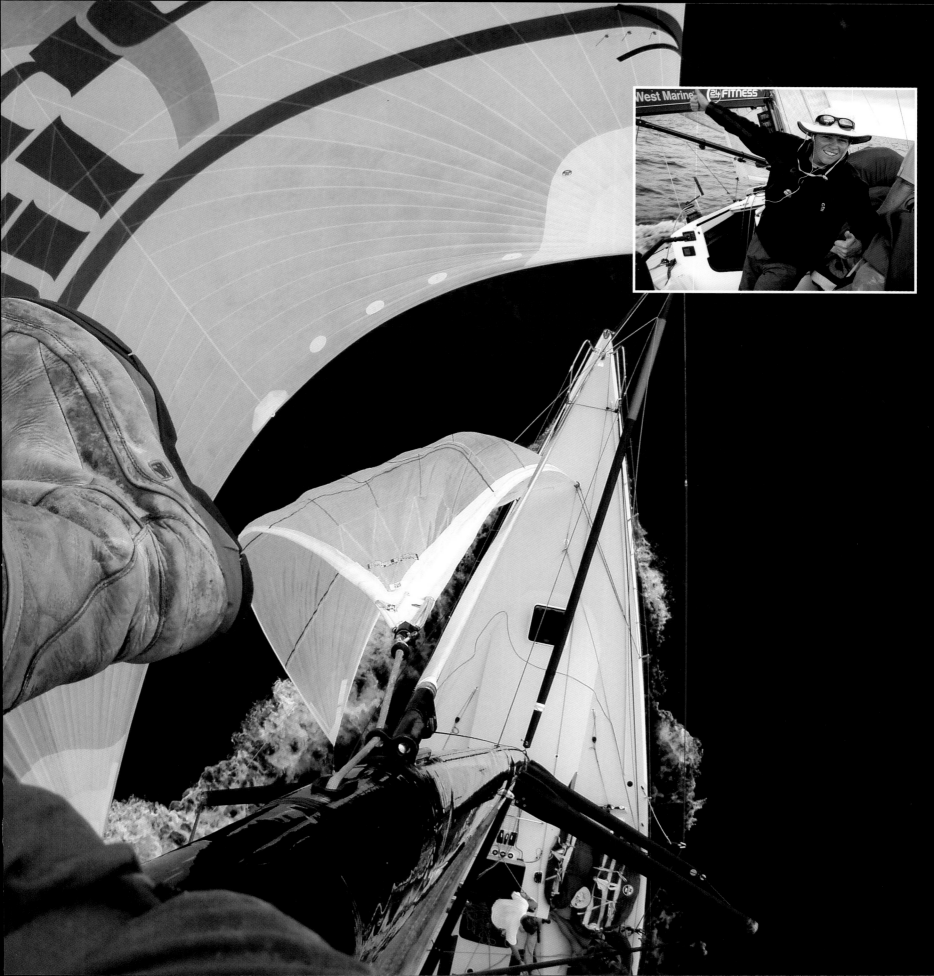

that was in the eastern lobe of the high. By the time of our start, that light air area had moved far enough south so that it was feasible for us to sail over it.

"In working with the kids we discussed that the northern course would likely be more appropriate for *Morning Light* than it would be for *Pyewacket*, which was configured for a light-air downwind race, and the upwind work of the northern course would not suit her, whereas *Morning Light* and her crew were fully prepared for a long upwind thrash. Having completed the Molokai course three times and a trip to Hilo and back, all in over thirty knots, the 'kids' were well prepared to race upwind in a near gale.

"So the race initially unfolded very differently than we discussed. *Pyewacket* headed north, the kids headed south, the opposite of what both boats initially planned."

There has been no communication between *Pyewacket* and *Morning Light* since the start last Sunday.

"I was, and in fact still am, a bit concerned that the kids will be upset that I said that *Pyewacket* was going south and then instead headed north," Honey said. "On the other hand, I suppose that is why boats still carry navigators onboard so that they can evolve strategies as new information becomes available."

Honey also commented on the performance of Steve Manson, a *Morning Light* alternate who wound up on *Pyewacket*.

"We've had endless conversations onboard with Steve about the outlook for the kids. They have a real race on their hands with the guys on *Samba*.

"Steve is working on his bowman techniques with Jerry Kirby and Rick Brent and has also been adopted by the grinders. Steve is a natural athlete, and he only needs to see somebody do something exactly right once or twice and then he can nail it. Steve also keeps his eyes open the way many good sailors do and sees rigging problems early when working on the bow."

PREVIOUS PAGES: *Morning Light* and *Samba Pa Ti* match-race in the middle of the Pacific.
OPPOSITE: *Samba Pa Ti* trails just off the *Morning Light*'s stern.

It will be interesting to see how we do. They definitely have a faster boat than us. The only reason we've been hanging on is because Branning has been doing a really good job tactically. Hopefully, we can out-jibe them and keep them in some squalls. —**Kit Will**

It's the sixth day, and we've been racing pretty hard today. We've jibed on every shift that's favorable toward Hawaii and we're trying to get away from this dissipating high that's further north. We're really fighting to get south right now to get into more wind. So it's been a real physical day for everybody, and we'll probably continue on throughout the night. We still have Samba behind us—they kind of rolled us a little earlier this morning, and then we started to jibe south and started doing pretty well, being really aggressive, and finally they started to fight south too. We were able to come out ahead of it by a good bit, but they're sailing pretty hot right now. —**Chris Welch**

It's day six, early evening right now, and we're getting some better pressure. Everything seems to be going better and better, and we're heading south right now, trying to catch stronger trade winds. We've got Samba right here on the port side. We've kind of been dancing around with them all day. It's been pretty interesting—a lot of close match racing, which is weird for an ocean race to be this close for so long, but we're pushing hard. It's cool to look over your shoulder every now and then to see a really well sailed boat with really good guys and us, you know, being competitive with them, it kind of gives us a little bit of competitive morale boost, so it makes us work that much harder. —**Chris Schubert**

HONOLULU—All this year, Roy E. Disney's young *Morning Light* sailors have been trained not only how to race their Transpac 52 in the forty-fourth Transpacific Yacht Race to Hawaii but how to prepare it and, if necessary, repair it as well. The only thing they weren't trained for was what they've found themselves in the last couple of days: a match race way out there in the Pacific Ocean.

"I have heard people talk about sailing side by side with other boats in the middle of the Transpac," messaged Piet van Os, who is co-navigator with Chris Branning, "but I never imagined match racing *Samba Pa Ti*."

At times the two boats have been as close as three boat lengths apart, otherwise alone in the vastness of the largest ocean, an unlikely bout between *Morning Light*'s ocean-racing rookies and John Kilroy's partly professional team on *Samba Pa Ti*, also a TP52.

Meanwhile, Disney, ashore in Honolulu, was also tracking the other unfolding drama of *Pyewacket* chasing down the only six boats still in front of his ninety-four-foot super boat. All started three to six days earlier, and *Pyewacket* is virtually assured of the Barn Door for the fastest elapsed time. But finishing first, regardless of a head start, rates high in bragging rights in the beachfront bars along Waikiki.

Morning Light, with a crew ages eighteen to twenty-three, had its own hands full.

Van Os, twenty-three, of La Jolla, California, and a senior at the California Maritime Academy in Vallejo, said, "All the training in the past six months is all coming together as we race neck and neck with one of the best TP52 teams in the race. I have always wanted to race Transpac since I was very young and heard the stories of my grandfather winning in '61."

His grandfather, A.B. Robbs, Jr., sailed *Nam Sang* to first place overall on corrected handicap time in 1961, but Grandpa never told any Transpac tales like van Os has experienced.

"The first four days of the race were nothing like anything Transpac vets told us about—upwind in variable winds," Van Os said. "We started the race with the southern route in mind and sailed the first twenty hours racing south. After looking at the weather some more, we decided that there was a chance for us to minimize miles while sailing in the same amount of breeze as the southern route would have, so we headed north. The only comfort we had was that the rest of the boats on the northern route had the same or less breeze.

"Eventually the wind built and with it came the morale. We were off on port tack heading to the cold front we were expecting. We sailed into it enough to get the forty-degree right shift, a ten-knot breeze increase and heavy rain. After sailing through it, we were able to crack off and start heading toward Hawaii. On day four we were able to finally set a kite and, in our minds, the Transpac race had started.

"Day five brought the first sighting of a competitor since the start. *Samba Pa Ti* was behind us and working toward us. We sailed in sight of *Samba* for more than twenty-four hours, pushing the boat as hard as we could. At four a.m. on the twentieth we were just five boat lengths apart in an all-out drag race in the middle of the Pacific. We knew that *Samba* would be one of the hardest 52s to beat in the race, and to be right alongside of them after over a thousand miles of racing was an accomplishment in itself.

"Friday we split a bit as we pushed a little harder south. At six p.m. I went on deck to talk with the watch and saw our friend *Samba Pa Ti* taking our stern about a mile and a half away."

Samba Pa Ti owes *Morning Light* about one and a half hours in handicap time. The latter is slightly heavier, not counting cinematographer Rick Deppe, who is performing no crew tasks while filming the activity for the documentary theater film to follow.

"As for the movie side of things," Van Os said, "Rick has tried to capture the everyday life onboard. I'm no cinematographer, but this morning when the sun was rising astern of *Samba Pa Ti* just three boat lengths on our stern, it had to be an amazing shot! [Escort vessel] *Cheyenne* was also there just ahead of us, catching all the action. It had to be a funny shot if anyone else could have seen it . . . *Cheyenne*, *Morning Light*, then *Samba Pa Ti,* all in a line at six a.m. with the sun rising in the background all in the middle of the Pacific."

It's day seven here in the Pacific Ocean. After being out at sea for a good solid week, I definitely have some things running through my mind. And the one prevailing thing was that although this boat is such an awesome piece of technology, you still have one factor that the carbon fiber can't speak to. And that factor is definitely the human element. The human element that this boat has is incredibly special. It's an incredibly unique dynamic that's been forged over the last six months. And to be living this dream we've all had for the last six months is just incredible. —**Jesse Fielding**

We've got about a thousand miles left. And hopefully we'll take them off faster than the last thousand-plus miles because we'll be going downwind with the kite up. We have to take a pretty big detour to the left here to get around this big high-pressure system where there's no wind. So that's kind of a bummer. You would just want to sail straight to Hawaii. We're pointing at it right now. But you can't always do that.

I think the test of a really good team is a race like this where you're offshore. You go kind of crazy because of it being so long. And you all get a little testy. And if you don't know each other really well then you don't know when you're getting on someone's nerves. It's so easy for somebody to blow up or to get ticked off. So it's really good to have spent a lot of time with everyone here. I've been on boats where, you know, it's only four days and everyone's ready to kill each other by the end of the race.

So it's pretty clear that we're all having a good time. There's no real tension on the boat right now. We've kind of gotten into our rhythm. And we all just have the same goal in mind. We want to get to that town and buoy as quickly as possible. **—Kit Will**

July 22, 2007 – DAY 8

HONOLULU—A flying finish almost made the first half of the forty-fourth Transpacific Yacht Race to Hawaii forgettable as *Pyewacket*'s bid for the record fell 9 hours 7 minutes 44 seconds short Sunday.

Roy Pat Disney, co-skipper with Gregg Hedrick, described the race in brief as "frustrating and exhilarating . . . and sad."

A record wasn't in the wind.

The race's other remaining drama continued far at sea with the two Transpac 52s, *Morning Light* and *Samba Pa Ti*, still locked together in a match race on their own little pond. Sunday morning's roll call reports showed *Samba Pa Ti* slightly south and still within sight of *Morning Light* with a one-mile lead.

So we just got the report from Branning. And it's pretty favorable. On one hand, we worked really hard last night to get south, flying the shifts downwind. We had a period of about ten jibes where we were definitely making ground. We did really nice things on Holua. They had to come south, too. Everyone to the north does because of the high and the way the dynamic of a high works.

As you sail around a high-pressure system and the breeze shifts, the breeze angle is actually like a tangent to the circular high. So as you sail around this high you're just going to get lifted and lifted and wound into it. And then you'll never be able to get to Hawaii because it's just going to get lighter and lighter. So the guys to the north had to start working south. And we just did a really nice job of doing that. We were really aggressive with our driving and playing the shifts. Samba's still out in front of us physically, but within eyesight, so nothing too big to report on that front. **—Jesse Fielding**

One of our little hobbies that we've kind of picked up is talking about the instantaneous cravings that we have. We've got a lot of weird ones. Robbie Kane's got these deep-fried Oreos, coated in pancake batter, and a bunch of us are craving Reese's and different types of pizza. And Chinese food. So someone says, "Hey, who could go for this right now?" and everyone will kind of go to their happy places thinking about having a nice thick steak or blue cheese cheeseburger or something. **—Chris Schubert**

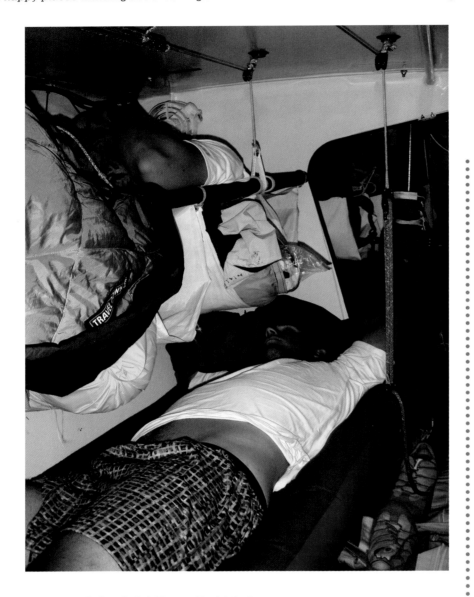

July 23, 2007 – DAY 9

HONOLULU—There was still considerable action at sea with a second match race between Cal 40s heating up to the level of the ongoing joust of Transpac 52s. Both were so tight that in each case the boat behind was ahead of its rival on corrected time—Steve Calhoun's Cal 40 *Psyche* over Don Grind's *Far Far* and the *Morning Light* rookies against John Kilroy, Jr.'s *Samba Pa Ti* pros. The TP52s should finish around midnight Wednesday, the Cal 40s the next day.

It's day nine and we've made like twenty miles in an hour and a half, which was great for us. So we'll finally get away from the light air, and being able to just rip along for a while is really fun. We've had some competitors around all day. We had Holua, who we've been fighting for first in our division. We saw them for a while this morning. We got the squall and they kind of didn't so we pulled away from them, hopefully.

Then we sailed through a couple of the Aloha class— cruising boats that left a week before us. So it's been cool just to be feeling like we're moving forward in the fleet. At least to have boats around us that we're doing better than or that we're faster than. We've also had our last day of real food, of three real meals, so we're all content right now and a little bit nervous about starting rationing tomorrow, but I'm sure it'll be fine.

Morale is good on the boat, we've got maybe two and a half, three days left, and we're all, you know, thinking about the food that we want or the people who we're going to see on the dock.

We're seeing some squalls line up already, so it's going to be dark pretty early and we're ready. We're ready for a big night of squalls, a big night of jibing, a big night of wind, and we've all been saying that for the last three nights, but it does really seem like it's going to start happening.

It's just fun that we're ticking down the miles. I don't know if that's good or bad to keep reading out how many to go, but we have less than six hundred I believe, so we're looking forward to just pushing really hard this last little bit and then finally making it, seeing the islands and getting to the Diamond Head buoy. It's going to be cool. **—Genny Tulloch**

As we've gone along and during this race, I've been continually impressed by Jeremy. Continually impressed by the fact that every thought of his is really concerned about boat speed. Sailing with him is kind of a joy. Especially racing. He keeps his mind on what's important, always looking for that last little ounce of speed. —**Chris Schubert**

 *Here we are on day ten, and we have a competitor five miles off our stern. We sailed five days next to Samba. This race has just thrown everything at us that it possibly could. A cold front in the Transpac, two stationary highs in the middle of the race course we had to get around. Match racing with Samba in the middle of the night. Now dealing with Holua. We're up against some of the greatest navigators to ever do this race. There's not been an easy moment.* **—Chris Branning**

HONOLULU—On day ten the Transpac 52 match between the young *Morning Light* team and John Kilroy, Jr.'s *Samba Pa Ti* turned weird. A questionable morning position report relayed from *Samba Pa Ti* by another boat indicated that the latter had broken away on a deep dive south in the past twenty-four hours and sailed 249 miles at 10.4 knots to *Morning Light*'s 201 at 8.4 knots—but lost thirty-three miles in distance to the finish, now 499 to 530 in *ML*'s favor.

That would place the boats about 165 miles apart on the course with *Samba Pa Ti* due east of Hilo on the Big Island, an unlikely position this late in the race. How that plays out will be known when they finish, probably late Thursday.

July 25, 2007 – DAY 11

HONOLULU—Going south late in the forty-fourth Transpacific Yacht Race to Hawaii has paid off dramatically in battles between classic boats of the old and modern eras.

Over a period of twenty-four hours Steve Calhoun's *Psyche* won a battle of Cal 40s, and a bold move by John Kilroy, Jr.'s *Samba Pa Ti* apparently put *Morning Light*'s rival Transpac 52 deep in arrears with only a day's sailing to go.

Meanwhile, Hawaii-based *On the Edge of Destiny*, sailed by five young men comprising the youngest crew ever to sail Transpac—average age 19.8—finished in the light of a bright three-quarter moon floating low on the horizon just after one a.m. Wednesday to claim a third-place podium finish in Division 5.

But it was Monday's brash call apparently by *Samba Pa Ti* navigator Nick White that caught everyone—especially the young *Morning Light* team and its shore supporters—by surprise. In Tuesday morning's roll call position reports, *Samba Pa Ti* was so far south that knowledgeable observers thought its posted location at latitude 19-21 east of Hilo on the big island was in error.

Nope, just a desperate but well-calculated end run to shake off *Morning Light* by sailing farther to gain leverage in stronger winds south of the usual path to Diamond Head. By Wednesday morning *Samba Pa Ti*, sailing two knots faster at 11.6, had gone from thirty-one nautical miles behind *Morning Light* to nineteen miles ahead.

Actually, they're competing for second place in Division 2 behind the current leader, Brack Duker's *Holua*, a Santa Cruz 70 to which the TP52s owe handicap time.

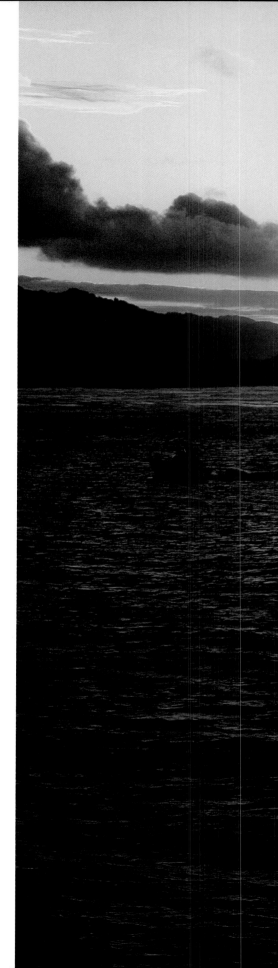

It's been a lot of fun. There's some fun moments, you know, in the big puffs. There've been some scary moments. There's been some pretty loopy moments where it seems like people need to get out of the sun a little bit and have a little bit more water.

But it's been a really great experience. A lot happens over the course of eleven days out so far from shore. It's amazing spending that much time within such a small amount of space. I mean, there's twelve people on this boat, and the boat is only fifty-two feet, so imagine being in a little bedroom with twelve people. You do a lot of rubbing shoulders with people. It gets kind of close, but you end up better friends because of it. **—Chris Schubert**

It's day eleven, and we're about twelve hours out from the finish, hopefully, if everything goes smoothly, and I think we're all pretty excited to be getting close. Everyone's working a little bit harder knowing that this is pretty much the end, and we can put 110 percent effort into it and not worry about burning out.

I'm in disbelief that the race is almost over. I think it'll be pretty shocking once we actually get there, to actually have finished the race and realize that this whole project we've been doing is coming to an end. But I think we've certainly all pushed the boat as far as we can.

We've been working every wave the whole way, and no matter what, we'll know that we put as much as we could into the race. And that was the goal. I think we've shown that we're a competitive team, and we definitely trained hard for it, so we're all excited to be getting to the end. —Kit Will

HONOLULU—Cameras ready . . . places everyone . . . cue sun . . . cue boat . . . action!

And so Hollywood came to Hawaii, or so it seemed Thursday as Roy E. Disney's *Morning Light* project reached its climax when the Transpac 52 of the same name sailed by its crew of sailors ages eighteen to twenty-three finished the forty-fourth Transpacific Yacht Race to Hawaii.

The year-long documentary from crew selection through the race is scheduled to hit the big screen in 2008, but who will believe the ending was for real? Sunrise was at 6:03 a.m. and *Morning Light* finished at 6:09 a.m. against a flaming orange backdrop of the eastern sky on a nautical set that even Tinseltown wouldn't believe.

"Honest, only God could do this at the finish," Disney said. "He clearly understood the title of the movie."

It hardly seemed to matter that another TP52, John Kilroy, Jr.'s *Samba Pa Ti*, had finished in the

dark more than four hours earlier to leapfrog Brack Duker's Santa Cruz 70 *Holua*, the Division 2 front-runner, for first place in the division, leaving *Morning Light* in third.

The younger sailors felt no disappointment—"None whatsoever," said Charlie Enright, twenty-two, of Providence, Rhode Island—and were happy just to have been in the hunt almost to the end.

Piet Van Os, twenty-three, of La Jolla, California, who teamed with Chris Branning, twenty-one, of Sarasota, Florida, as navigators, said, "The fact that we feel good is an understatement."

At Friday night's awards dinner they will share the podium with two strong teams of professionals, including world-class navigators Mark Rudiger on *Holua* and Nick White, who made the gutsy call that brought *Samba Pa Ti* a roundabout win. *Holua* finished less than an hour behind *Morning Light*, which owed it about three and a half hours in handicap time.

Kilroy explained *Samba Pa Ti*'s sudden detour: "We went on the great navigator Nick White's Pacific tour. Since our boat is optimized for higher speeds, we had to find wind. The wind was too light for our boat. Even still, it was fun to be out of the office."

White, a New Zealander with a strong ocean racing résumé, said, "We were sailing our own race. I saw the pressure and knew it was time to go. Some thought we went too far south, but it looks like it worked out."

Van Os said, "I was trying to think why they did it. We thought it was a flyer. We didn't think it was going to work. We saw it, but it looked too risky. But their boat reaches better than ours, so if I was in that position again I'd make the same call we made."

Morning Light was accompanied over the 2,225 nautical miles by *Cheyenne*, a 125-foot power catamaran—formerly Steve Fossett's sailing *PlayStation*—carrying a production team.

Kilroy said, "We were all impressed with the kids on *Morning Light*. Obviously, they are talented and were well trained . . . although it was actually quite distracting at times having such a large escort vessel

around. In an ocean race you're used to being out there alone. We were glad when we turned down.

The *Morning Light* sailors enjoyed the mid-Pacific competition while it lasted.

Mark Towill, a native Hawaiian, said, "One morning we woke up, and they were two lengths behind us. It's a crew full of professionals who have gone around the world and stuff."

The *Morning Light* team averaged 21.2 years in age, which put them in step with the local *On the Edge of Destiny* team of five young men averaging 19.8 years that placed third in Division 5 a day earlier as the youngest team ever to sail Transpac.

The *Morning Light* skipper was Jeremy Wilmot, a twenty-one-year-old Australian who was elected to the position by his American peers.

"That was the longest, hardest, struggling, stressful thing I've ever done in my life," Wilmot said. "But at the end of the day I loved it."

Morning Light made an unusual zigzag move of its own when after passing the Koko Head peninsula near Diamond Head it turned into shore, then jibed and sailed back out before jibing again to finish. A cynic might have thought the youngsters were playing to the two helicopters and various photo craft recording their every move for the documentary.

Wilmot explained, with Aussie humor, "We thought we'd get killed by the production team if we ruled out finishing with a spinnaker."

Van Os said, "We learned when we were training here for four months that usually you get good puffs coming down that valley, but they weren't there so we went back out."

Robbie Haines, Disney's longtime *Pyewacket* sailing manager who doubled as *Morning Light*'s head coach, said, "They practiced that."

Jesse Fielding, twenty, of North Kingston, Rhode Island, said, "Awesome trip. The team we formed over the last six months came together, and we're going to stay together."

Genny Tulloch, twenty-two, of Houston, Texas, the only woman on the boat, said, "For me, being an ocean racer is a whole new world. I grew up in dinghies. It's a different language. I didn't even know what a '[spinnaker] peel' meant. Hopefully, I can be a role model to show anyone can do it."

Haines: "It's way beyond my expectations how well they did and how well they got along."

Disney: "It's not about how they did. It changed people's lives. They've all gone through a life-changing transition."

That's a wrap.

9

The Finish Line

Recollections and Reflections from the *Morning Light* Crew

Aug. 1, 2007

HONOLULU—Transpac 2007 epilogue:
The forty-fourth Transpacific Yacht Race to Hawaii had seventy-three starters, the fourth-most ever; the youngest crew (*On the Edge of Destiny*, average 19.8 years); the oldest crew of two (*Tango*, each age seventy), and the oldest boat (*Alsumar*, seventy-three years).

It also had the fun-loving Webster brothers from Oklahoma sailing a fifty-two-foot luxury catamaran, *The Minnow*, while puffing on sousaphones and playing Beethoven sonatas on an electric piano the whole 2,225 nautical miles, and a team of young sailors recruited and trained for the sole purpose of sailing the race while a production team recorded their every move and sound to make a documentary film about it.

It was a good year for Australians. Jeremy Wilmot, twenty-one, was elected skipper by the *Morning Light* crew and led them to third place overall in Division 2.

Morning Light, a Transpac 52, has been sold to Syd Fischer, Australia's living legend of sailing, who plans to race it in the Sydney-Hobart classic starting December 26, 2007 (Boxing Day). He hasn't named a skipper, but Wilmot might be available. His parents would never have let him sail the Sydney-Hobart. They might see it differently now.

Crossing the Diamond Head buoy was a sign of relief for me. It was the first time in eleven days that I could sit back and take a deep breath, bend my knees, and let go of the wheel. It was too much to handle at the time, crossing that line, there were just so many mixed emotions. I didn't know how to feel. Leading up to the mark, I just wanted to push the mark further away. I wanted to add miles to the race. I almost wished we were going to Japan instead of Hawaii to keep the journey going.

But at the end of the day, we set off to race to Hawaii as fast as we could, and to win the race. We finished the race. We didn't win the race, but we rattled some cages, and we showed everybody out there what a group of young, determined, twenty-one-year-olds are capable of. **—Jeremy Wilmot**

It's been so hard to put this whole program into words. It's like trying to describe a sunset or a sunrise or trying to describe what the stars look like at night. You have to be there. You have to experience it. Only then can you start to grasp what it was like. **—Chris Branning**

Transpac 2007 Final Standings

In order of corrected handicap time (place in total fleet in parentheses).
All times by days:hours:minutes:seconds.

ORR rating allowances in parentheses; time allowance subtracted from elapsed time to determine corrected handicap time.

Division 2 (Started July 15)

1. *Samba Pa Ti* (Transpac 52), John Kilroy, Jr., Los Angeles (2:04:02:17), ET 10:15:565:55, CT 8:11:54:38 (24).

2. *Holua* (Santa Cruz 70), Brack Duker, Pasadena, California (2:08:51:12), ET 10:21:10:00; CT 8:12:18:48 (26).

3. *Morning Light* (Transpac 52), Jeremy Wilmot, Honolulu (2:05:27:19), ET 10:20:09:13, CT 8:14:41:54 (28).

4. *Skylark* (Santa Cruz 70), Doug Ayres, Newport Beach, California (2:06:24:05), ET 10:22:13:44, CT 8:15:49:39 (29).

5. *Hugo Boss* (Volvo 60), Andy Tourell, Gosport, UK (1:23:10:32), ET 10:16:59:05, CT 8:17:48:33 (31).

6. *Westerly* (Santa Cruz 70), Thomas and Timothy Hogan, Newport Beach (2:06:06:45), ET 11:03:00:27, CT 8:20:53:42 (35).

7. DH-*Pegasus* 101 (Open 50), Philippe Kahn/Richard Clarke, Honolulu (2:00:47:54), ET 11:00:26:56, CT 8:23:39:02 (37).

8. *Lucky* (Transpac 52), Bryon Ehrhart, Chicago (2:05:26:28), ET 11:10:38:40, CT 9:05:12:12 (44).

9. *Trader* (Transpac 52), Fred Detwiler, Pompano Beach, Fla. (2:09:31:32), ET 11:18:29:22, CT 9:08:57:50 (47).

Complete position reports: www.transpacificyc.org

Afterword

Fair Winds and Following Sea

A Farewell from
Roy Edward Disney

It has been said, "A sailor without a destination cannot hope for a favorable wind." We had a destination in mind at the beginning of the *Morning Light* Project, but to us, the more important thing was the journey. As with any voyage, there were eddies and doldrums, squalls and storms, but in all, we arrived where we intended to, blessed by the sea with different results than we had wished for—but far more rewards than we had hoped for.

Of course I wanted them to win, as they all did, and it would be disingenuous to claim otherwise—and anyone who's been sailing as long as I have who says they don't care about the win, or the broken record, is being just a bit dishonest.

When I did this thing the first time, it changed me for the rest of my life—but I don't think I knew that at the time. I think it kind of comes to you later on, and you have a resource that you can look back on and say "You know, in hard times, I dealt with life, and I dealt with it well and gracefully," hopefully.

That's what it really means in the end.

One day we were all sitting around in the living room at the Crew House, and I happened to be sitting next to Genny. She looked at me and said, "What's the thing that surprised you most about this whole deal?" I said, "All fifteen of you. Because, you know, we started with a blank slate. We didn't know who you were going to be—and you have turned out to be the most wonderful group of kids I've ever been around in my life." I want to adopt all fifteen of them. That's probably not legal.

During the race I watched those kids every day, sweating out every hour, and talking about their decision-making process onboard, and I was enormously pleased with the decisions they made. They've clearly not only made good decisions but have been making them gracefully.

That part of it fascinated me because it is exactly what you hope will happen with any group who have been trained and have been working together well, thinking together well, and coming to the right conclusions—together.

And I really believe their lives have already been changed.

I think any one of these kids can get a ride to just about anywhere on anybody's boat after this experience. Which of them will want to, and which of them will want to have different lives beyond this certainly is up to the individual. I know there's a few that would really like to become professional sailors. There's going to be doctors and lawyers and all the rest in there, too, but they'll have an experience that will help them in whatever they decide to do.

In the end, I can only hope that what they will remember and treasure is not their destination, but their journey.

—Roy E. Disney

Rachel
Levy

MISSION TO MADAGASCAR

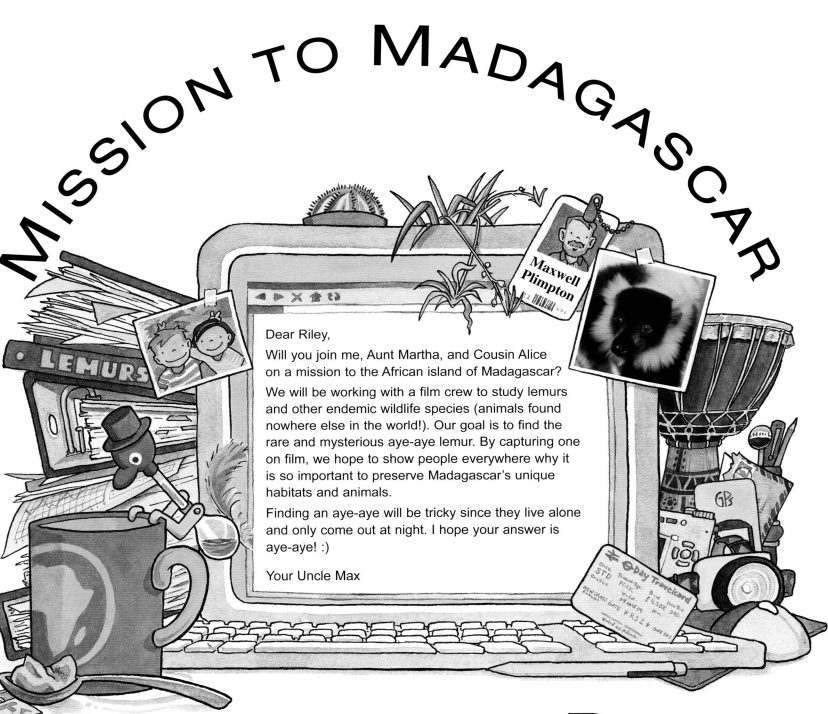

Dear Riley,

Will you join me, Aunt Martha, and Cousin Alice on a mission to the African island of Madagascar?

We will be working with a film crew to study lemurs and other endemic wildlife species (animals found nowhere else in the world!). Our goal is to find the rare and mysterious aye-aye lemur. By capturing one on film, we hope to show people everywhere why it is so important to preserve Madagascar's unique habitats and animals.

Finding an aye-aye will be tricky since they live alone and only come out at night. I hope your answer is aye-aye! :)

Your Uncle Max

Maxwell Plimpton

LEMURS

ADVENTURES OF RILEY

BY AMANDA LUMRY
& LAURA HURWITZ

Eaglemont
Press

ILLUSTRATED BY
SARAH MCINTYRE

Photo Credits:
cover baobab tree © Loren Dolman/PONDARAY
title page black and white ruffed lemur © Andy Rouse/NHPA
pgs. 4-5 baobab alley, pg. 9 painted mantella, pg. 19 Parson's chameleon © Martin Harvey/NHPA
pg. 6 tourist bungalow at Perinet Reserve, Madagascar © MCarol Polich/Images of Africa/AfriPics.com
pg. 10 black and white ruffed lemur © Martin Harvey/AfricPics.com
pg. 12 leaf-tailed gecko © Kevin Schafer/NHPA
pg. 13 Madagascar foliage © Nigel J Dennis/Africaimagery.com
pgs. 14-15 Perinet reserve, pg. 16 indri in tree, pg. 17 crested coua © Nigel J. Dennis/NHPA
pg. 16 rufous ground-roller, pg. 17 Madagascar boa, pg. 19 giraffe-necked weevil, pg. 20 fossa female, pg. 29 aye-aye © Nick Garbutt/NHPA
pg. 17 diademed sifaka with baby © Peter Oxford/NaturePL
pgs. 18-19 Madagascar foliage © Nigel J Dennis/Africaimagery.com
pg. 20 tropical rain forest tree © Nick Garbutt /NaturePL

Illustrations ©2005 by Sarah McIntyre
Editing and Finished Layouts by Michael E. Penman

Digital Imaging by Embassy Graphics, Canada
Printed in China by Midas Printing International Limited
ISBN-13: 978-0-9748411-2-0
ISBN-10: 0-9748411-2-9

A special thanks to all the scientists who collaborated on this project. Your time and assistance was very much appreciated.
Additional thanks to Royal Botanic Gardens, Kew, for use of its library and for its research material on Madagascar vegetation.

A portion of the proceeds from your purchase of this licensed product supports the stated educational mission of the Smithsonian Institution - "the increase and diffusion of knowledge." The name of the Smithsonian Institution and the sunburst logo are registered trademarks of the Smithsonian Institution and are registered in the U.S. Patent and Trademark Office.
www.si.edu

2% of the proceeds from this book will be donated to the Wildlife Conservation Society.
http://wcs.org

A royalty of approximately 1% of the estimated retail price of this book will be received by World Wildlife Fund (WWF). The Panda Device and WWF are registered trademarks. All rights reserved by World Wildlife Fund, Inc.
www.worldwildlife.org

First edition published 2005 by
Eaglemont Press
PMB 741
15600 NE 8th #B-1
Bellevue, WA 98008
1-877-590-9744
info@eaglemontpress.com
www.eaglemontpress.com

Library of Congress Cataloging-in-Publication Data

Lumry, Amanda.
  Mission to Madagascar / by Amanda Lumry & Laura Hurwitz ; illustrated by Sarah McIntyre.– 1st ed.
      p. cm. – (Adventures of Riley)
  Summary: Riley, Uncle Max, Aunt Martha, and Cousin Alice travel to Madagascar, where they encounter a variety of unique animals, plants, and habitats while searching for the elusive aye-aye, a rare lemur once thought to be extinct.
   ISBN 0-9748411-2-9 (hardcover : alk. paper)
   1. Aye-aye–Juvenile fiction. [1. Aye-aye–Fiction. 2. Lemurs–Fiction. 3. Zoology–Madagascar–Fiction. 4. Madagascar–Fiction.] I. Hurwitz, Laura. II. McIntyre, Sarah, ill. III. Title.
   PZ7.L9787155Mis 2005
   [Fic]–dc22
                                         2005001350

"I can't believe I'm going to Madagascar to look for lemurs," said Riley.

"Elephants and lions, too?" asked Mike.

"Probably, but we'll be looking for a rare lemur called the aye-aye that only comes out at night," said Riley. The thought gave him the shivers.

Uncle Max and Aunt Martha greeted Riley at the London airport.

"Is that Alice?" Riley asked.

"She thinks this is her chance to be a movie star," chuckled Uncle Max. Alice glided over.

"Hello, darling! Do you like my new look?"

GATE 14

TIME NOW : 13:52

DON'T GET STUCK IN TRAFFIC
TAKE THE TRAIN

SOUVENIRS

SCOTTISH WOOLIES

HOLIDAY OFF—

BOOK

Antananarivo – Ivat—

"Are we there yet?" grumbled Alice, after they landed in Antananarivo, Madagascar's capital.
"Almost, but first we have to pick up the film crew in the Spiny Forest," said Uncle Max.
"Then we'll go to our lodge in the East Central Rain Forest."
"How about some tasty kitoza and rice porridge for breakfast?" asked Aunt Martha. Max nodded enthusiastically.
"I'm too sleepy to eat," yawned Alice. Riley agreed.

3

Baobab Tree

➤ This tree looks like it is growing upside down, with its roots in the air!

➤ It can live for several thousand years.

➤ Bats and lemurs pollinate the tree.

➤ Sometimes its trunk is wide enough to be used as a house.

Laurence J. Dorr,
Associate Curator, Botany,
National Museum of Natural
History, Smithsonian Institution

"Are those things trees?" asked Riley.

"Yes, these baobabs survive the dry desert climate by storing water in their trunks," said Aunt Martha.

"There's the film crew!" Alice squealed. She tossed her feather boa over her shoulder and dashed out to meet them.

"I'm Brigitte and this is my husband, Carlos," the woman said.

"It's going to be hard to leave these beautiful trees," said Carlos.

"They're amazing," gushed Alice.

As if you even noticed, thought Riley.

At the lodge, they were met by a man named Jaona. "When does the filming begin?" asked Alice.
Before anyone could answer, Aunt Martha lifted a huge insect out of Alice's hair. Alice screamed.
"It's just a hissing cockroach," said Aunt Martha. "They make great pets."
"Your rooms are this way," said Jaona. "You must be tired from your travels."
"I could use some beauty sleep," said Alice.
"I don't think sleeping will help,"
laughed Riley.

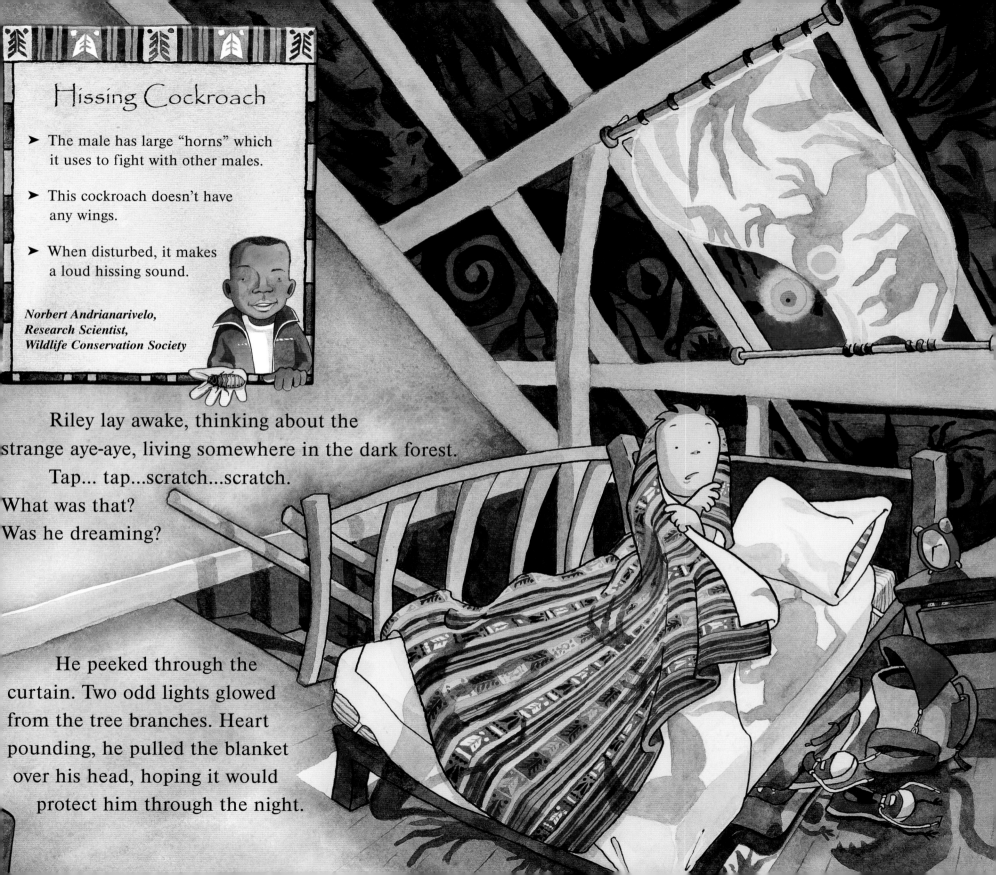

Hissing Cockroach

➤ The male has large "horns" which it uses to fight with other males.

➤ This cockroach doesn't have any wings.

➤ When disturbed, it makes a loud hissing sound.

Norbert Andrianarivelo,
Research Scientist,
Wildlife Conservation Society

Riley lay awake, thinking about the strange aye-aye, living somewhere in the dark forest.

Tap... tap...scratch...scratch.

What was that?

Was he dreaming?

He peeked through the curtain. Two odd lights glowed from the tree branches. Heart pounding, he pulled the blanket over his head, hoping it would protect him through the night.

"Get up, lazybones!" cried Alice, yanking off Riley's covers. "The film crew is waiting!"

Downstairs, nothing could get Uncle Max and Aunt Martha out of bed. Opening one eye, Uncle Max groaned, "I feel awful."

"Maybe we shouldn't have eaten that kitoza," said Aunt Martha.

"You and Riley will have to go without us," said Uncle Max.

"No problem!" said Alice.

8

Painted Mantella Frog

➤ The male makes very loud call sounds.

➤ The female can lay up to 27 eggs at once.

➤ Yellow, green and black coloring usually means that it's poisonous. Don't touch!

Don E. Wilson, Senior Scientist
Smithsonian Institution

Black and White Ruffed Lemur

➤ Rain is no problem for this lemur. It has long, waterproof fur.

➤ It is found very high up in tall trees in the rain forest.

➤ It is the only lemur that makes a fur-lined nest.

Vanessa Rasoamampianina, Research Scientist, Wildlife Conservation Society

Their first sighting was black and white ruffed lemurs leaping from branch to branch.

"Most lemurs are arboreal. That means they live in trees," said Brigitte.

"Aye-ayes are arboreal and nocturnal, so we probably won't see any until after dark," said Alice, leaning against a tree.

"Carlos, zoom in by Alice!" said Brigitte. Alice struck a pose.

"Stay still, Alice, or you'll scare the leaf tailed gecko," said Carlos.

"The what?" asked Alice. The gecko's skin exactly matched the color and texture of the bark.

Leaf Tailed Gecko

➤ This gecko has a flat tail and body.

➤ During the day, its iris becomes a very small vertical line to help keep sunlight out.

➤ The edges of its skin lie flat against the tree, making it difficult for predators to see.

Achille Raselimanana, Biodiversity Programme Officer, World Wildlife Fund Madagascar & West Indian Ocean Programme Office

42

That night, Uncle Max and Aunt Martha still felt sick, so Riley and Alice grabbed their headlamps and once again joined Carlos and Brigitte.

"Where are you going?" asked Jaona.

"To look for aye-ayes," said Alice.

"Many local people believe aye-ayes are a sign of bad luck, so they kill them on sight," said Jaona.

"We've heard that," said Brigitte. "We hope our work will show that aye-ayes are important to Madagascar, and that not seeing them would be far more unlucky than seeing them."

In the dark, the forest seemed to close in around them. Riley and Alice followed Brigitte and Carlos...a little too closely!

They didn't spot
any aye-ayes, and
Riley was glad.

The next morning, Uncle Max and Aunt Martha woke the children. "Hear those indris?" Uncle Max boomed. "Time to get up! That's your Madagascar alarm clock!" Uncle Max made up for lost time by opening up the forest to them.

Rufous-Headed Ground Roller

➤ It hides in the deep shade, making it hard to spot.

➤ It loves to sing and can often be heard on forest walks.

➤ It builds its nests on the ground.

Dr. George Powell, Senior Conservation Scientist; Suzanne Palminteri, Senior Conservation Specialist, World Wildlife Fund

Indri

➤ It sings one song each day to communicate its territory. The song lasts from 1 to 4 minutes.

➤ The Malagasy named it *babakoto,* which means "father of a little boy". That is because its call sounds like a father searching for his missing son.

Aleta Quinn, Research Collaborator, Smithsonian Institution

Madagascar Tree Boa

➤ It hunts for small animals or birds using a heat-sensitive gland on its snout.

➤ When a female is pregnant, her skin will darken to help absorb more sunlight for warmth.

Herilala Randrimahazo,
Research Scientist,
Wildlife Conservation Society

Diademed Sifaka

➤ Its hind legs are strong and long, so it can jump from tree to tree.

➤ Its only predators are human and the fossa.

Dr. Sheila M. O'Connor,
Conservation Measures and
Audits, World Wildlife Fund
International

Blue Coua

➤ It is related to the cuckoo and is only found in Madagascar.

➤ It gets its name from the color of the skin around its eyes.

➤ A female lays only one egg at a time.

Dr. Nancy J. Clum,
Assistant Curator, Ornithology,
Wildlife Conservation Society

"Uncle Max, I thought we were going to see lions and elephants in Africa," said Riley. "Where are they?"

"They don't exist here and never have. Instead, the island of Madagascar is home to many unique animals that cannot be found anywhere else. That is why it is often called the eighth continent."

"Max!" interrupted Carlos. "That Parson's chameleon has one eye on you and one eye on its supper!"

Giraffe Weevil

➤ There are 60,000 different kinds of weevils, making it the largest animal family in the world!

➤ It is 3 inches (80mm) long.

➤ Eggs are laid in wood. Once hatched, the young tunnel and feed.

Gary Hevel,
Public Information Officer,
Smithsonian Institution

Suddenly, the chameleon's tongue darted out and snapped up a nearby giraffe weevil.

"Did you see the size of that weevil?" Aunt Martha asked.

"All I saw was that long slimy tongue," said Alice.

"Slimy, but useful," said Uncle Max. "Did you know chameleons communicate by changing color? Green means calm, and yellow means angry."

Parson's Chameleon

➤ Some local people believe it is poisonous to the touch, but this is not true.

➤ It can rotate one eye at a time, and can look in two different directions at once!

➤ A male can grow to be 27 inches (695mm) long.

Jim Murphy,
Herpetologist Emeritus, Smithsonian Institution

"If I were a chameleon, seeing that strange dog over there would make me change to whatever color means *scared*."

"And for a good reason," said Aunt Martha. "That's a fossa, not a dog. It is the island's largest predator and it can jump and climb trees."

"They hunt lemurs, including aye-aye," said Uncle Max.

"Oh no," said Alice.

"But fossas aren't their biggest threat," said Uncle Max. "They are most threatened by humans and invasive species, animals which were brought here from other countries. Farmers cut and burn trees that are home to lemurs and other wildlife so they can plant crops and raise zebu cattle or other non-native animals. Eventually nothing grows. The ground washes away, so farmers must clear more of the forest."

Fossa

➤ It is a shy animal that prefers to be active at night!

➤ While it looks like a cat, there are no wild cats on Madagascar. The fossa is more closely related to the mongoose.

➤ It can climb trees, which helps it to catch lemurs.

Dr. P.J. Stephenson, Coordinator, Africa & Madagascar Program, World Wildlife Fund

Madagascar

➤ It is the fourth largest island in the world, about the same size as Oregon and California combined.

➤ The baobab tree is its national symbol.

➤ Eight out of every ten creatures in Madagascar exist nowhere else on earth.

➤ Ninety percent of the island's original vegetation has been cleared.

Yvette Razafindrokoto,
Research Scientist, Wildlife Conservation Society

Uncle Max chose their path that night. Riley wanted to hold his uncle's hand, but he didn't want anyone to know he was scared.

"Uncle Max, the lemurs we've seen look friendly and cuddly. What is so different about an aye-aye?" asked Riley.

"It's the size of a cat," said Carlos.

"With ears like a bat," said Aunt Martha.

"Plus a long furry tail and sharp teeth like a squirrel," said Brigitte.

"And a long bony finger like a skeleton!" said Alice, poking Riley with a stick.

Uncle Max put his arm around Riley. "Listen, Carrot Top. Aye-ayes are funny looking, but they are nothing to fear. They won't hurt you, plus their round eyes glow in the dark, like night lights in the forest."

"Thanks, Uncle Max,"
sighed Riley, smiling for the first
time all night. Aunt Martha hugged him.
"Riley, never be afraid to tell us you're scared." They searched
late into the night, but didn't see any aye-ayes.

25

26

Riley woke up suddenly in the dark. He pulled open the curtain to let in some moonlight. Again, he saw two small glowing lights. Grabbing his flashlight from under his pillow, he gasped. Next to a nest of twigs was...an aye-aye?

27

Riley woke the others and rushed outside.

"Is everything okay?" asked Jaona, running up the path.

"Would you look at that?" said Uncle Max.

Jaona froze.

"It *is* strange looking, but really not too scary," said Riley. "Just think of it as a night light!"

"Okay," said Jaona, nodding slowly.

Aye-Aye

➤ The aye-aye's sharp hearing helps it find grubs crawling in dead wood.

➤ Its long, bony middle finger lets it spear grubs and insects deep inside the wood and pull them out.

➤ It is not a picky eater, eating insects, nuts, eggs and even honey.

Steven Goodman,
Coordinator of the Ecology
Training Program, World
Wildlife Fund, Madagascar

The aye-aye scratched the
tree limb using its finger, pulled out
a fat grub, and popped it into its mouth.
"Not exactly movie star behavior,"
said Aunt Martha.

Suddenly, the camera light came on and Carlos and Brigitte were right there, filming away. Alice smiled. "You know what, Mum? For this movie, I'd say the star is behaving perfectly."

"Thanks to Riley," said Uncle Max, "our mission to capture an aye-aye on film has been accomplished. It's amazing that they were once thought to be extinct. Now we can show that there is hope for the aye-aye...and hope for Madagascar."

Back at school, Riley explained that while Madagascar had no lions or elephants, it had quirky creatures that existed nowhere else and were in danger of not existing at all. He told them all about the hissing cockroach, the leaf-tailed gecko's camouflage and the aye-aye's moonlit munching.

He returned to living the life of a nine year old... until he got his next letter from Uncle Max.

Where will Riley go next?

Further Information

Rachel Levy

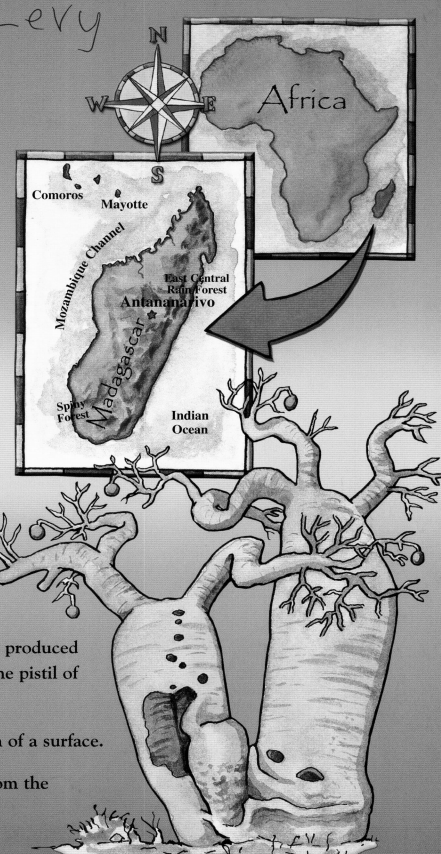

Africa

Comoros
Mayotte
Mozambique Channel
East Central Rain Forest
Antananarivo
Madagascar
Spiny Forest
Indian Ocean

Glossary:

CONTINENT: A large land mass, such as Africa, Antarctica, Asia, Australia, Europe, North America and South America.

ENDEMIC: Something that is from a given area. (Not foreign.)

HEADLAMP: A light attached to a band that is worn around one's head.

INVASIVE: Something that is not from a given area. (Foreign.)

KITOZA: Dried beef, usually served with rice porridge.

NOCTURNAL: To be awake and active mainly at night.

POLLINATE: To take the fine dust produced in seed plants from the stamen to the pistil of the flower so that it can bloom.

TEXTURE: The feel and/or pattern of a surface.

WEEVIL: An insect from the beetle family.

WHAT IS THIS?

➤ Hidden inside each *Adventures of Riley* book is at least one compass.
➤ Each one will unlock an on-line Further Adventure movie on Riley's website.
Visit Riley's World today!
www.adventuresofriley.com